ADVANCE PRAISE

"DeLuca debuts with a surreal ride through the supernatural history of the city of Detroit and the strange territory of new parenthood. Aileen is a recent transplant to Detroit and a single mother of a newborn. Her neighbor Virgil is the only person she's grown close to since the move, so when he asks to borrow her bicycle so he can participate in a semimythical monthly bike ride called the Night Roll, a riff on the folkloric Wild Hunt, she feels obligated to say yes. When Virgil doesn't return, Aileen becomes desperate enough to venture out to find him, bringing baby Christian with her—and stumbles into a small but generous community of Detroit locals. In the process of earning their trust, Aileen gets many lessons on local history, learning about the Rebellion (also known as the '67 riots) and the Elf, the ageless trickster who leads the Night Roll. The odd, lyrical story meanders, propelled only by the force of Aileen's determination to take control of her life—a determination that culminates in the reality-bending Halloween Night Roll. The result is a hypnotic near-future novella that will captivate literary and genre readers alike."
Publishers Weekly

"DeLuca's deft, poetic eye keeps hope right where it needs to be, not as magic, but as imperative, creative power."
ZZ Claybourne, author of *The Brothers Jetstream: Leviathan*

Night Roll

This is a work of fiction. All characters, organizations, and events portayed in this novella are either products of the author's imagination or are reproduced as fiction.

Night Roll

Cover design by Anne Middleton

Edited by Selena Middleton

Published by Stelliform Press
Hamilton, Ontario, Canada
www.stelliform.press

Library and Archives Canada Cataloguing in Publication
Title: Night Roll / Michael J. DeLuca
Names: DeLuca, Michael J., 1979- author.
Identifiers: Canadiana (print) 20200233432 | Canadiana (ebook)
20200233483 | ISBN 9781777091729 (softcover) |
ISBN 9781777091736 (ebook)
Classification: LCC PS3604.E5483 N54 2020 | DDC 813/.6—dc23

For my partner and my kid

NIGHT ROLL

Michael J. DeLuca

Stelliform Press
Hamilton, Ontario

1

Nursing half-naked in a salvaged rocker in the loft at Holden and Trumbull, watching through the triple window as mid-summer night slipped past vacant lots and vacant buildings, Aileen saw the first bike go by silent and so faintly glimmering she didn't know it was real until long after. Christian's hot mouth at her nipple was the only thing keeping her awake. Christian might have been two months old. Aileen hadn't seen Andrew since the hospital.

Can you call them dreams if you know you're awake?

Their last real conversation came back along with his shape against the green-gray windows, his hand on her hip, his smile with too many teeth. She thought he'd been stoned, tripping.

It'll be fine, all this will pass.

For you, it will. But she couldn't muster the energy to hate him. Not now.

Then, now: Virgil's voice through the door. "Hey lady, you awake?"

A car went by, one of the autonomous ones, recognizable as much by the incongruence of its presence as by its spectral bullet shape jarring over potholes and high, faint hum. No car that expensive ought to come this way ever. Something wrong with its AI.

Christian slept, their little mouth still working. Dreaming of Andrew? She laid them down, brushed sweat from their brow, went and whispered through the door. "What time is it?"

"You watching? The window, they coming, look." Virgil was her neighbor three lots up among the abandoned houses on Marquette — her only neighbor, for all she saw the other tenants in the "revitalized" lofts along Holden.

"Who?"

"They follow the Elf," was what she thought he said, voice raspy from cigarettes and squatting in an unheated house through winters. Maybe Virgil was wake-dreaming too. "Aileen," he said, "I got to ask a favor. Let me borrow your bike."

Her bike: it hung clipped to the wall by the door, royal blue, chrome and leather, custom, not ostentatious, too beautiful to let languish outdoors for all these months she couldn't ride it. Fourteen speeds, disc brakes, cargo mountings, touring rims, racing bars. She'd traded slick tires for knobbier ones since fleeing the East Coast for Detroit, better for these rotten roads. Riding had been dangerous for Christian then. Now it was more so.

She rested her forehead against the cool door. He'd sleep-ride it somewhere and forget. He'd ride it away and never come back.

"Hey, lady, listen — how many times I come visit in a day?"

Lady: she understood it as a term of endearment. It sure wasn't about her money, or her age. She'd saved enough not to be in utter panic about being alone and unable to work; the months would count down, she'd stay on her budget and try not to think.

"Every day," she admitted. Virgil had been an auto worker. She didn't know what he did now. Nothing? He brought gossip she didn't understand. He'd brought half-melted soft serve, an electric fan, the cast-iron washbasin she was using as a bassinet. So heavy he might have killed himself wrestling it up the stairs.

"You know why?"

4

"No, why?" *Because I let you in the first time. Because you're bored.* Because he wanted something, and now she knew what. What she loved most in the world, aside from the little blob of poop and tears dozing in the washbasin.

He made a hurt sound. "Trust me. I'll bring it back. I know it's important to you. You know most people don't hang their bikes on the wall?"

That made her laugh a very little, very quietly.

She let him in out of the stairwell, checking late that her breast was covered — that wasn't what he wanted.

Virgil dressed, always, like he'd been getting ready for a marathon for thirty years: ancient blue hoodie and sweats, pristine sneakers. He smiled a lot. He smiled, his teeth glowing in the half-light.

She put a finger on her lips. He put one on his. "You want it *now?* What for? Do you even know how to ride?" She winced as the words came out of her mouth: patronizing.

She guessed he was used to it. "I want to go with them. To see what they see."

Christian shrieked in their sleep as Virgil led her to the windows.

"Who?" she said again, not awake, but then they came.

There were no stars, no moon, just the shield of citylit haze. Outside the derelict-bank-become-dive-bar, one of the streetlights worked. Through its glow, cyclists flickered, aglow themselves — bikes and bodies, bare skin and spokes wound with lights. Hiphopified soul thumped through the windows, muddy freestyle in the breaks. Virgil fidgeted, a cat watching birds through glass.

Watching him, Aileen felt conflicted. She knew about trapped. Andrew had taken the car; it was his car. The bike had been her way to move through this empty city; now she couldn't use it.

Someday she'd need her bike. Now, she needed a friend.

Christian burbled, coughed. She scooped them up before they could start to scream again.

She flicked the light switch by the door and found her purse by the harsh light from the neglected kitchen. She'd been living off frozen casseroles. This had been the plan. It was working. But it was awful using the oven in this heat. "You can borrow my bike," she said, "if you'll take it to Eastern Market and buy me vegetables."

Virgil nodded solemnly. "Of course, lady." This time it was almost courtly. "Thank you." Thinking of fresh basil, of Andrew shirtless on the rooftop misting young tomato leaves with compost tea, she showed Virgil how to unclip the bike from the wall, gave him the helmet, lock, and key.

Before she could show him the patch kit and tools under the seat, before she could lecture or warn him, he was spilling down the stairs, the bike over one shoulder. And Christian needed to be changed again.

❦

Day was like night, just hotter, brighter: changing, feeding, crying, wake-dreaming, sleepwalking. They cried together: Aileen for her bike, for Andrew, for herself, for her life as it had been; Christian for unlife, for the womb, for loneliness and grief at having only Aileen.

We can live in the ruins, grow food, and make art, Andrew told her. *We'll save so much money. It's not like anyplace else is hiring.*

She dream-hallucinated fucking him, being oriented to him at the base of her spine; inside her, he made them a triangle, she, him, the baby. The unborn Christian became their center of balance, then threw them into a death spiral. But before that, Aileen would have sworn she could see their future, the austere urban ruins sprouting new gardens, new life, and she'd wanted it, wanted him. Her stretched crotch ached.

Night Roll

She woke from forty-five minutes' blissful sleep to momentary, visceral lucidity. Four hours past noon, the loft air hot and close. The fan whined desperately.

Virgil should have been back. Days this hot, Eastern Market closed early, all that brick and pavement. Stupid, she didn't have his number. She wasn't sure he had a phone.

She was gasping, suffocating.

She gathered Christian and carried them down the dark stairs. Sun and heat off the crumbling pavement like a wall. She was risking their sensitive skin, their new eyes, their first time outside since the hospital. She tottered back upstairs and got a damp tea-towel to shade them. She needed this.

She splayfooted around the corner up Marquette. At Virgil's, she wasn't stupid or lucid enough to risk the steps to the door with the faded white paper in the window that meant *CONDEMNED*.

Across the street, a couple vaped on an unruined porch. They exclaimed over Christian and invited her into their shade. "He went with all those bikers —" Aileen said, "— cyclists," fanning Christian and herself with the tea towel, dragging a slick hand across her brow like a debutante. The woman, Gladys, offered her a glass of powdered lemonade from under a floppy hat with a fake rose. Pale scars decorated Frank's cheeks; he blew cherry-flavored vapor politely away and wore a device to track his vitals. "Virgil? Haven't seen him today."

Sparrows fought in a black walnut tree, wing, beak, and talon, as she splayfooted back to the loft. A plane gleamed in a bare sky. Out of the heat Virgil appeared, walking her bike, a bag of beautiful fresh greens slung on the handlebars. *It was all I could carry.* He smelled like beer, sweat, early raspberries, and spilled gasoline. She blinked and he was gone.

She interrogated his lingering vision in her kitchen. Virgil's tracksuit was torn at the knees, the skin dark with blood. A grown man wobbling all over the road like a kid with the training wheels off. "When was the last time you rode a bike?"

He didn't know.

"Then what did you want it for?"

Don't you ever just want a change? He laughed. *Supposed to be like riding a bike.*

She could have strangled him. Or at least sponged the blood from his knees.

She drank from the tap, ran it over Christian's bare legs to cool them. Their huge dark eyes saw what she couldn't.

"What was it like?" she asked Virgil's shade.

It's a big city. You forget. Walking, you hardly get anywhere. Take the bus, it's like you're just passing through. Feels different on two wheels. Felt like a kid again. Felt old as the Elf, too, seeing everything that's changed. Old ruins, sure — been in ruins since I was young — but new things springing up. Gardens. Money. New, old. He shook his head.

The Elf?

She couldn't get on a bike for at least another month. She couldn't take Christian with her for four. Four more months. She itched for the escape, the sense of movement, of freedom. Even in a month, who could she leave Christian with? Virgil.

She fed Christian. She thought of Virgil holding them. *Easy,* he said, *like a dough on the rise.*

She made a chalky smoothie with protein powder, flax seed, frozen peas. She stood at the foot of the ladder on the landing, sipping, feeling neither human nor awake, gazing up through the ceiling at the dead container garden.

When she found out she was pregnant, Aileen gave up alcohol, weed and coffee. She gave up biking. She insisted, out of hope for some kind of vicariousness, that Andrew do nothing of the kind. "One of us should drink," she said, trying to be funny, to put a good face on. Andrew resisted, then gave in.

And then spiraled? He'd stay on the rooftop for hours, where she could no longer go, and what could she say? He talked about dreams, waking dreams, about visions for the future, and of the past, and of riding the crest of a wave leading all the time from one to the other. Maybe it was that their lives had changed so much so suddenly. Maybe he'd always been like this, maybe pregnancy was making her crazy.

❦

She let another night pass in fits of not-sleep, helpless to stop it. Christian would never grow or change, was incapable of it. She watched for the horde of cyclists, she listened, but the street stayed quiet except for a half-dead Dart coughing up its lungs at three-thirtyish, and then — again? A teardrop-shaped Cadillac, undriven, to the thump of a familiar sample. Didn't have to be the same one; there were plenty.

Virgil's shade took her bike and left. It dawned on her he'd been the only adult she'd talked to since the hospital. Frank and Gladys made three.

She had to get out of the house. Even if it could be dangerous for Christian, she had to get out. They were so young. But if she stayed she'd go crazy. She might hurt them, might let them get hurt.

She packed spit-up cloth, diapers, pacifier, water, toys, a jar of pickles from what little was left in the fridge. She put on an enormous-brimmed gardening hat that would cover them both, and went across the street to the bar.

The Marble Bar was marble like the thick, windowless stone of the abandoned bank building it occupied, not like a blue-green cat's-eye marble rolling along Holden and all the abandoned arteries of Detroit, unscarred by potholes, not slowing. A flyer on the door said it didn't open until three. Another flyer advertised something called Night Roll, the moon a bicycle wheel emerging from occlusion behind an art deco skyscraper. She took this flyer and took Christian home out of the sun.

She waited, sweating, dozing, changing, crying, feeding.

❧

The bar was cool, air-conditioned, not empty a minute past three. Aileen levered herself and Christian onto the stool closest to the door, propped her flip-flops on the rail, blinking in the dark.

"Night Roll," said the bartender, tall, with an eloquent nose and a neat, dark beard, who made Aileen's libido swish and smack. She was losing her mind, she'd lost control of her body. "They do it every full moon."

"This says May and October."

"Couple times a year a bunch of bike shops and the city cycling advocacy get together and sponsor it. Then they get a police escort, t-shirts, flyers, people come in from the suburbs. Usually it's a lot smaller."

"Like the other night?"

"I was working." He placed in front of her a tall, skinny glass of ice and cucumbers, condensation dripping down the sides, slow fizz rolling upward. "It's not alcoholic," he said to her desperate stare. "These are kind of my specialty, actually."

She sipped. "Omigod."

He leaned his elbows on the bar. "She's cute."

Aileen looked at Christian. Their eyes remained clearer than the clearest pre-pre-predawn sky since their birth. They were some kind of prehuman cosmic intelligence sent to feed on her life force, to doom her, but yeah. Cute.

The bartender, seeming to take the hint, retreated to the dark end of the bar to serve something that wasn't his specialty.

The flyer was blank on the back. On the front, just a website and some social media come-ons. "The full moon's not for weeks," she called, over a dub heartbeat. "How do I get in touch with the organizers?"

The bartender came back, made her repeat it. He was extremely accommodating, and very handsome.

You don't want to find out what's down there, she wanted to tell him. Or maybe he was just taking pity. She gritted her teeth, clung to the baby for strength. The words came fast, a bitter pill. "I'm new here, I'm alone, I don't know anybody."

He recovered. "Uh. Block party in Corktown this weekend?" He wiped his hands on a towel, got a pencil, and wrote on the back of the flyer an address, a date, a phone number. "It's a community thing, totally safe. I could take you? Introduce you around. Bartending's good for that, I know everybody." He leaned across the bar, smiling, easy, reassuring. She must have looked scared. "I'm Omar."

Bags overflowing with kale did not appear overnight. Her bike did not appear. Virgil did not appear. She couldn't live on bespoke cucumber mocktails even if she'd wanted to give Omar the wrong idea, so she lived on frozen casseroles, frozen soups, frozen stir-fries. She could make it to Saturday. Not that there'd be anything to help her make it past that.

When she ran out of patience babbling at Christian, she tried talking to Virgil. It was weirdly diverting.

A concrete block church, said his ghost, *no windows, padlocks on the doors. A brick and stained-glass church with wire over the glass, doors hanging open. Miles of potholes, cobblestones crumbling, underpasses hub-deep in gray water. Gray clouds rising from under the street. Women in hijab picking wild onions in vacant lots. A house on fire with nobody around. Loved, lived-in neighborhoods, kids shrieking in sprinklers. A mirrored tower of glass. Cadillacs. Telsas. F350s. LeBarons. Murals. Broken windows. Burned timbers. Tags. Fries, exhaust, sunhot tar, cut grass, spilled alcohol, spilled gas. Bikes going by fast, riders hunched pumping in dayglo spandex with logos. Bikes going slow, riders half-*

walking, plastic bags hanging off everywhere bulging. One lone old bike, weaving, rider ragged, no helmet, long hair matted gray not moving even in wind, knees akimbo, not looking left nor right, not for traffic or nobody. Humming a song with no tune. No matter how hard anybody ride, can't seem to catch up.

She asked herself where it came from and had no answer. The place dreams come from, the place they're supposed to go when you're awake.

Saturday came. She knew because she'd been counting. She packed a bag and carried Christian in her arms down to the bus stop at Trumbull and Grand.

She waited almost an hour, automated cars going by, zip, zip. Should have walked the whole way. But it was hot, and there was Christian. She'd never make it.

On the bus, Andrew sat across from her, long, sinewy in a pale suit and green tie. He'd lost weight, gotten taller. From under his endearing, infuriating curls and scruff, he looked at his tablet, never at her, nodding to music so loud she could hear it through the earbuds — thrash or something — concentrating so hard crows' feet constricted the corners of his eyes. They were the only two on the bus.

She lunged across the aisle and yanked out the earbuds, electrified. "Stop blocking us out," holding Christian between them like a talisman.

It wasn't him. She retreated in shame.

She kept her senses enough to notice when the bus passed a parking lot strung with red flags, full of people. Street signs: Virginia Park, then Euclid. She got out the flyer, turned it over to the address in Omar's smooth handwriting. She pulled the cord. The bus stopped; she stumbled to the door.

On the sidewalk she kissed Christian's cheek, held them close.

She sat on a bench and fed them, listening to hip-hop maxing out the PA, breathing shallowly the smells of grilled meat, trying not to feel sick. Bikes lined the sidewalk, chained to the fence, and people strolled past and in through the gate. She recognized Virgil's neighbor Gladys in a huge flowered hat, blocky heels percussing among a gaggle of older women. Aileen put away her nipple, to Christian's protestations, and made herself follow them. "Excuse me," she mustered.

She showed them the flyer; they looked past it at her miraculous fragile mercurial child.

"Isn't he sweet?"

"He's so tiny!"

"What's his name?"

They asked where she lived and for how long and whether this was her first and how old and where was his father, and Aileen wilted like unwatered basil under their regard. They took her inside to where the drinks were, in drums packed with ice in the hot shade of a blue awning beside the pavement "stage." She refused a cheeseburger, accepted a soda, pressed the cold can to her head and to Christian's chubby arms. Christian's eyes widened. The women exclaimed at their beauty and clarity.

She saw Omar, dancing among childless young people of the kind she had been. She waited, then when the song ended tried to make her way through the crowd. But he was gone, and she retreated to the meager shade, Christian heavy in her arms. The women introduced her to old men with sweaty bellies and smart-mouthed kids in too-big clothes. She was offered another burger, a hotdog. She was hungry, not hungry enough. Everybody apologized, all the corn was gone, she should have come earlier. She accepted a bag of barbecue chips, washed them down with cloying sweet soda. She realized the music was live only on being introduced to the MC. Reg "the Redeemer" pushed sweat off her brow into gray braids and regaled Aileen with a story everyone else already knew well enough for call-and-response: a one-hit wonder, the neighborhood anthem, a glimpse of that old Motown mint that had lasted half a summer and subsided. Aileen shook her head;

she didn't know it, wasn't one of them. Reg took up the mic again to show her. Everybody danced.

They reminisced. They'd had friends, lots of friends, they'd been happy, the city had been better, worse, they'd been angry, they'd struggled, they'd gotten beaten down, they'd endured. It seemed important, like it might explain why there was still a neighborhood here at all. She was tired, she lost the thread.

She blinked. There was Omar again. She excused herself, feeling unnecessarily guilty — everyone had gone back to dancing.

He looked surprised. "Aileen, right? I didn't think I'd see you. And this is —?"

"Christian."

Omar had his arm around a man. The other man was even taller, tattooed. He caught some hint from Omar and faded respectfully out of earshot, which wasn't far. Still, Omar had probably not been flirting with her.

"What am I doing here?" she said blankly.

"What?" Omar came almost close enough to make her second-guess.

"Meeting people," he prompted. "So you're not so isolated." She winced at this truth, and from behind his neat beard, Omar gave her a frank look, as if unsatisfied at having scried it. "Also, you were asking about Night Roll." He pulled the other man closer. "Morris, this is Aileen."

The two of them, tall and impeccable, looked down at her like puzzled, benevolent eagles.

"Can I hold her?" said Omar.

"Actually," Aileen heard herself say, "for now, Christian is a they."

"Ah, right," said Omar, as if he'd said "of course", so she was unable to say no. She started in about supporting the head and then saw he didn't need to be told, no more than Virgil. Christian's burning, small weight lifted away, then they were gazing quizzically up at Omar from the crook of his arm, their head against his bicep.

"Good luck figuring all this out," Omar told them, looking into their eyes, gesturing to everything: the people, the sky, the crumbling parking lot, Aileen. "We could use the help."

Aileen thought about Christian figuring any of it out. Growing up. She thought about them dating, having decided to be a boy, a man, and making a decision the opposite of this one Omar seemed to be making so flippantly because he only had to make it this once, to be nothing for a child who had everything to learn.

She folded down to the weedy pavement, hugging her knees not to burn her thighs, and tried to breathe.

The block party whirled around her. She wanted to sleep.

"You should ask Morris," said Omar presently, stooping down so she could hear.

She looked up and saw how he and Morris had taken positions upstream and downstream of her, making a calm eddy amid the flow of the crowd. "Ask him ...?"

Morris was still. Omar shuffle-danced, Christian in his arms. "Morris doesn't miss a lot of Night Rolls. Even in winter." Aileen realized she could have divined this from the shape of his calves, even if his ink hadn't included a bike with sunflowers for wheels. "He works day shift, for one thing." Omar, very plainly, was in love with him.

"I love it," said Morris, almost apologetically. "It makes me feel ... connected? You should try it."

She accepted a hand to her weary feet. As soon as I can ride again, she didn't say. "I lost a friend," she said. "He took my bike. He said something about an Elf and then he went. It was, like, three in the morning. That was a week ago. He was supposed to bring food."

"Six days ago?" said Morris, reeling back.

"I don't know. Yes?"

"What did he look like? Tall guy, tracksuit?"

"Uh, yeah?"

"To be fair," said Morris, "it wasn't like he blended in."

"What happened?"

15

"He fell." Reg the Redeemer freestyled murkily; Aileen had to strain to hear. "Not bad, but it could have been. At first I thought he was drunk. But then … he went right up to the Elf. Caught him up and rode with him. Like it was easy."

Aileen could measure time by the sweat droplets gathering mass in her collarbone, or she might have read cold in Omar's shiver. Christian gave that interrogative cry Aileen associated with being overwhelmed at reality. "I'm here, love, I'm here." She got up and took them. She really needed to sit down, lie down, fall down, eat something. "Did you see where they went? Who the fuck is the Elf?"

Now Christian was crying. Aileen forced herself to dance.

Morris said, "I don't feel qualified to answer that." He looked at Omar. "I mean, no, I didn't see where they went."

Omar, she thought, looked like he'd blundered into an intimate relationship with a single mother he wasn't remotely interested in sexually, and was only suddenly realizing that entailed a certain amount of obligation. "Okay," Aileen snapped, knowing it wasn't his fault, struggling and failing to restrain her tone, "so who's qualified?"

※

Who was qualified turned out to be Reg, the MC, the Redeemer.

"The Elf's just a legend," she was saying, with a dismissive wave of a newly empty mason jar, with her feet up on the ice-filled drum that held the keg. Aileen had been vouchsafed a seat close beside her, under the blue awning, surrounded by neighbors, admirers, hypewomen. She nursed Christian some more, not caring anymore who got a look. Her nipples were cracked, and it hurt. At least there was shade. At least there was ice. She kicked her sneakers off and followed Reg's example, pressing bare feet against the cold drum. Morris had disappeared. Omar was working the keg.

"So tell it," said Omar, smiling, refilling the Redeemer's jar with red beer.

He knew this crowd, he knew Reg, because they were ready to back him, catcalling, goading, a pattern prearranged. It made Aileen feel even lonelier. Her head swam. She tried to listen.

Reg kicked back, king on her folding-chair throne. "Put it this way. The Elf, they're like Billy Beaurein: old as dirt, never see him around. But he's got his hands in everything."

Laughter, encouragement. "Beaureins," Omar explained to Aileen, who was lost, "don't own as much as they used to. Oldest money Detroit's got left, I guess. Older than Ford. Lot of what they've got left must be falling apart. Billy Beaurein in particular." He looked to Reg for confirmation.

"Now, don't let me bad-mouth the Elf like that." She slugged at her beer. "They're older, way older, but they can still ride that bike. And they never had money." She swung legs to the ground, looked around at the big-hatted ladies, the big-bellied old men, the young couples sweaty from dancing, drinks in hand, the kids hanging off at the far end of the lot trying to mimic her flow. She gestured with her glass, up, past them, past Corktown's crumbling, muraled brick and the art deco facades of downtown, to the phallic complex of mirror glass towers standing apart from the rest at the river's edge, reflecting the blinding sky.

Andrew had commuted to those towers every day. Maybe he still did.

"It started right there," Reg said. "Lot of shit under the bridge since then, but take all that away. You can't — try any-way. When the French, the first white people came across the river to Detroit, the Elf was waiting. Little wild thing up high on the bank, throwing Black Bottom muck in their faces when they try to land their canoes. They retreat. Plenty of other places to plant their French flag, upriver and down. None of

17

them empty. Cadillac, he's not about to let it go. Let one red Indian make an ass of him in front of his men? Plus, the Elf's on the highest ground they've seen for miles, you know, strategic. So he leads a charge, fixed bayonets, for God and Louie. They get shit thrown in their faces, but it's not that high a hill. They make it to the top. And there's no Elf, nobody. Nothing but a creepy old burial mound with a view. Windsor and Belle Isle, all forests, fields. Little lines of smoke from three Native fires. Eagles and herons hunting catfish in the channel. Cadillac, he's got no fucks to give about the dead. No fear except of humiliation. Such a good piece of ground, that's where they build the fort, right there. Corner of Woodward and Jefferson."

Quiet, this time. Reverence, maybe? Heads shaking. Then after a minute somebody turned up the PA.

"Is that it?" said Aileen. Everybody understood something she didn't.

Reg shrugged. "How much more you want?"

"Tell what happened to Cadillac," said Morris, who'd been there after all, on the hot baking ground at Reg's feet, knees to his chest, like a kid at story-time. But his voice was cold.

"You all want a little more?" said Reg, and it worked, call and response. Aileen voiced her tiny yes like she was part of something. The music got low again — not gone, but just a drumbeat and a trill. She caught Reg touch an invisible hat to the DJ.

Omar went back to pouring beer.

"Cadillac's men, these are some of the best trackers in the world. Coureurs des bois. Iroquois mercenaries, some of them. Stone cold. But other than mud in their eyes, disrespect ringing in their ears, they can't find a sign this Indian was ever there. They rape and pillage, bring the Natives to their knees. But the rumor persists. A shadow, a smear on his name. The Red Elf, the French call him. Cadillac offers a bounty for his scalp. Doubles it. Nobody ever collects.

"Couple years later, the fort burns to the ground. Word gets back to the French crown Cadillac's come unhinged, abusing his power, bent on revenge against nobody, a ghost. Remember, this is seventeen-oh-four: slavery's legal, rape is official business, germ warfare gets a motherfucker promoted. Reprimand is a month away, minimum, orders from on high more like six. Got to be some serious shit, you're going to abuse power hard enough to actually get prosecuted for it.

"He spends four months in jail. Then he's out, exonerated, promoted. Crown names him governor of his home province back in France, he dies of old age, at home, rich. Hated by everyone who ever knew him, but so what? Now what's making me think of old Billy Beaurein again?"

"What about the Elf?" said Aileen, amid ooohs and oh noes of appreciation.

"Oh, they're still around, or so they say." Reg shook her head. "Yeah. Even unto this very day. Keep coming back, making trouble, making people in power look like fools. For what that's worth." She slowed a little, leaning into the beat, voice thick and deep, and the crowd leaned with her. "*Starting parties, starting fires, planting gardens, stealing tires.* The Elf's this city's patron saint. Everywhere you look, native Detroiters losing out, no matter how hard they hustle, over and over from that day to this. We're not going anywhere, neither is anybody else. Scare them off, they retreat to the suburbs and take the resources with them. Got to learn to live with them somehow." She glanced at Aileen a little too pointedly. "Omar, pull me another beer if you please? I got to piss."

Trying to understand what she'd been told, what it meant, Aileen became gradually aware again of the heavy, pulsing pressure of Christian's gums, rhythmic and persisting though there was no milk left. She gently pulled away from their mouth, eliciting a cry. Aileen slugged at her can of lime soda, already warm, and cried a little herself.

Omar primed the keg. Morris lay back on the burning asphalt, hands behind his head, looking up. Cold.

Michael J. DeLuca

Aileen nudged him with her toe. "Are you okay?"

Omar shook his head warningly.

Morris lay there a minute longer, then bolted upright. "No. Nothing. She's right, it's what the Elf is for. The myth, I mean. She gets the gist — it's just the details."

"Like what?"

"Like they didn't 'bring us to our knees' for another hundred and fifty years? Cadillac wasn't even the first white man in Detroit, he was just the biggest asshole. Champlain was here a hundred years before."

"I'm sorry," said Aileen, dismayed. "You said you weren't qualified —"

He shrugged it off. "It's fine. Nobody is."

She blinked, and everything was different. Morris was leaning over her. She'd been asleep, right there on the radiating pavement, Christian in her arms. "I don't exactly feel like dancing anymore," Morris said. "You want me to walk you to the bus?"

She'd done a dangerous, stupid thing, falling asleep with the baby in her arms in a plastic chair in a baking parking lot full of people she didn't know, except for Morris and Omar, who she'd only just met, who had every reason not to be there when she awoke. But they were, tall and bemused and benevolent. On impulse she asked them to dinner.

❦

"I had my bike back, and I was riding alone. It was dusk. A damp wind. At first I couldn't remember where I was going. Then it came to me: the backyard of a cathedral, fenced in with chain-link, all overgrown with fox grapes and bittersweet. I was supposed to meet someone. Someone important, someone I cared about.

20

"The streetlights were coming on. And I had that feeling you get — a kind of detachment from everything? Nobody could bother me, nobody could catch me, but I was part of this place I was riding through. I could smell the smells, I felt the heat.

"I miss that a lot.

"I crossed this broad, empty street into a neighborhood lined with old trees. There was a house that looked like it had imploded, then one that had burned, then one all fortified with block glass and iron cages over the windows. Deep shade.

"I caught up to Christian, and they were older, a little blond kid kicking along on one of those bikes without pedals. They wouldn't notice me, they kept looking at something further ahead. I wanted to ask — how did I miss this, what happened, were you all right growing up, who took care of you? I was afraid they might not even remember me. But then a big truck came up behind me, a blast of wind, and when I looked again Christian was gone. It was such a terrible feeling. Lonely. I was so afraid for them. But also — this is awful — I was relieved. And I hated that, so I kept searching for them.

"There was someone still ahead.

"I came out of the neighborhood onto another main road, and this one was busy, with headlights rushing past too close. A neon corner store, a graffiti-covered warehouse, an empty lot. New condos behind a fence. Then the river, and the island beyond. I knew where I was, and I kept expecting the city, downtown rising up — but it didn't. There was no freeway, no parking garages or casinos.

"Then I was riding on wood — like on a railroad bridge, you know, but this was the whole street. It was smooth, nice, but hard to control — I had to slow down. And then I stopped in front of a church. The brakes worked great.

"I couldn't tell if this was the church. There are so many. But I could see a long way down Jefferson, and this was the only one in sight. Simple, brick, with a white spire. I couldn't see Christian anywhere, but there was this strange bike lying by the doors.

"So I went up the steps, and the doors were swinging closed, and I caught them. They were heavy."

It was the first dream she remembered since Christian was born — at least aside from the hallucinations. "I know nobody wants to hear about other people's dreams. I know it doesn't mean anything. It just made me feel ... weirdly like myself again." She laughed, embarrassed.

"Maybe someday you'll get a good night's sleep and we'll meet the real Aileen," said Omar — gently, laughing with her. "In the meantime, I'm happy playing with your kid." He had each of Christian's pudgy fists wrapped around a finger and was walking them on undeveloped feet back and forth past the fan. He paused, bending his tall frame further to babble into the whirling blades, which threw the sounds back with a metallic stutter.

Christian did not laugh, only looked puzzled, lost, struggling to hold up their head.

"No, it's actually really interesting," Morris said, not looking up, focused on the chef's knife. He'd brought a cornucopia of veg: beans, mushrooms, tiny sweet tomatoes, zucchini, enormous prehistoric heads of kale, masses of basil and mint, an entire braid of garlic. Prepping stir-fry was like cutting their way out of an edible forest. "That's what Night Roll is like sometimes. The times I've seen the Elf."

Omar had told her, before she'd asked, that Morris's father had been Grand Traverse Band Odawa, his mom was Scottish, that his family was from "up North"; nobody from either side lived in the city anymore, except him. "And finding out that much was like pulling teeth. I'd let it alone." She'd tried not to let it affect her impression of him. He was quiet, until he wasn't. Perhaps a tiny bit obsessive — not in a bad way, just — focused?

"Sunflowers," he said, when she asked about his tattoos, "are basically weeds. They're native, you can eat the seeds, you can use the hulls to make dye, they're tall, they follow the sun. Seed position in the flowerheads follows Fibonacci and the golden ratio. And their roots produce a compound that inhibits the growth of a lot of other species. Not all. But a lot."

This was her life now. She had friends, a bartender and an urban farmer; she was getting to know them. All it had taken was Andrew going away and Virgil disappearing and Aileen nearly suffocating with loneliness until she got desperate enough to leave the house.

And Christian. Who was not yet a person after two months, who did not know how to laugh. First, they'd have to accumulate some small experience of human interaction. Aileen found herself yearning for this future Christian, no longer in this post-gestational interstitial noplace, but fully present, a person, an ally.

It might, she knew, go nothing like that. Christian would choose their own identity. That was the point. Aileen would have to be patient, wait and live and be a person for both of them, for Christian to feed from, learn from, for months and months, maybe years to come. To manage that, to survive it, she needed friends. And here were Morris and Omar, asking in exchange only her trust and the chance to play with her child. Finding them seemed the latest in the wildest run of roller-coaster luck that had ever struck her. It was enough to make a person believe in karma. But not in fairies, not quite.

She was washing oyster mushrooms, cool water running over her wrists, thick air moved by the fan brushing over the back of her neck like leaves. The mushrooms were like ears, like Christian's ears if Christian's ears were gilled, pale, and profuse, insectile faces peeking from among them. Her eyes fluttering. She snapped them wide. Dangerous. What if she'd been holding a knife? What if she'd been holding Christian?

Morris had been saying something. She took a breath and a sip of Omar's fauxjito — even more amazing than his virgin gimlet. "I'm ... sorry, what? What do you mean?"

Then Omar was at her elbow, smiling, Christian in his long arms. "Trade me jobs? I'm no chef, but I can take direction, trust me."

He winked. Morris reddened. She hadn't figured out the dynamic between them.

"What I mean is," Morris said too loudly, then checked himself, "in your dream, what makes you think that was Virgil you were following and not the Elf?"

Aileen took Christian's small, too-warm weight from Omar and cradled them to her chest with a kind of relief. "Thank you. I'm — yeah. Still really tired." She sank down in the rocker, an involuntary sigh. "You don't need direction, it's a stir-fry."

"At least supervise?" She assented with a wave to being humored, and Omar pulled the rocker, Aileen and Christian in it, around to the side of the island where she could see. "What goes in first? Garlic?"

She shook her head, rocking gently. "Pan hot as you can stand it. Sunflower oil, dry spices just until you can smell them, then beans, garlic, then everything else except the basil and cilantro right at the end. Morris, you were saying ... what are you saying? That it was a true dream? Like, a prophetic dream?" She laughed nervously.

Deftly, Morris scooped bean ends between one palm and the knifeblade into the compost.

She shook her head. "Wasn't that your point when Reg told it at the block party? The story stays around because it's something people need, not because it's literally true. Because ... it's a story about fighting hard against ridiculous odds, and losing, but having a sense of humor about it?"

Omar nodded sagely. Christian burped gently and beat an impotent fist against her collarbone.

"You don't have any reason to think otherwise," said Morris. "You've never seen him. If you had it would be different."

"Has Reg?" she asked.

He moved on to thin-slicing garlic. He was fast.

"She's been to Night Roll," said Omar, clicking on the heat. "She loves it. But when she's there, it kind of tends to be about her. Any excuse to flaunt it, you know? She's a storyteller."

"Whether she believes or not," said Morris, "she benefits from placing herself opposed to him. Playing one story off another. The Elf is one genius of subjugated Detroit, she's the other."

"The Rebellion versus the hustle?" said Omar. He'd pronounced it with a capital R.

"What's the Rebellion?"

He gave her a startled glance. "Sorry. Forgot you're not from here. It's the word people here use for what everybody else calls the '67 'riots'. You should probably work on that. Some people ... Black people, intellectuals ... Reg in particular ... can get pretty hurt about it."

"Oh," said Aileen. "All I knew about the riots — the Rebellion — was that they happened. The army got called in?"

"And parts of the city never came back," said Omar grimly. "You're fine, you didn't know. Just — you might want to read up. I can lend you a book, if you're interested."

"Thank you for telling me."

"Nobody told me about it 'til I went to college," Morris said, transferring knives and cutting boards to the sink.

"Why would they?" Omar asked, and again Aileen felt that stiffness between them, and again she wasn't sure how to ask.

"Anyway," said Morris. "Next Night Roll's in a couple weeks. You coming?"

She nodded. "Of course, I wouldn't miss it." Exhausted as the prospect made her.

"So I guess we'll find out then."

Omar, sweating already, flicked water into the pan; it disappeared with a hiss. "Okay — spices, then garlic?"

"Spices, beans, then garlic."

Christian was searching for a nipple. Aileen pulled aside her tank top, grateful it could be now instead of during dinner.

The loft filled with the smells of ginger, cumin, and cinnamon, then garlic.

Heat, flavors, textures, structure, time. It was second nature to her now, after plenty of mistakes. The only wild card this time was some new drought-tolerant variety of brassica — between broccollini and rabe, Morris had assured her. It would work out or it wouldn't. Next time she'd try something else. Low stakes. Not like raising a child by herself in a new city.

They were good friends. Generous, forgiving, funny, and strange. She wanted to thank them, had thanked them already. She didn't want to seem desperate. She thought about the future, about living here, growing into this place and these friends, while Christian grew up. Grew to think of this place as home. The child Christian would be gangly and pudgy by turns, would walk, would wander the rotted pavements and pick weeds, make friends with strangers. Aileen would get them a bike, the kind without pedals to teach balance, and Christian would learn, and sail along sidewalks at risk to life and limb, they would fall and get scrapes on pink baby skin, they would cry, Aileen would comfort them. "It's okay to fall," she'd say. "Everybody falls, everybody makes mistakes."

They had to wake her again for dinner.

2

Aileen put Christian in their swaddle carefully under the mail-boxes at the bottom of the stairs, then went back up and dragged the rocker down, bump, bump, bump, along with the diaper bag and a blanket she couldn't imagine needing, to be safe. The breastfeeding pillow she lost off the top of the pile, so then back up to retrieve it, bringing Christian, because they were fussing. Then up and down one last time, feeling like the ferry oarsman in the riddle, having forgotten the enormous smoothie cascading sweat over the kitchen counter.

She flomped into the rocker, pressed the cold flask of smoothie to her temple, and looked up at the full moon. It was red, but she didn't put any stock of superstition into that. Her tiny family cluttered the sidewalk like too-loved trash awaiting a city hauler that would never come.

She wouldn't have thought of this moon as a milestone at all if they weren't sitting out under it, this ineffable, question-able presence at the head of a caravan of fairy-lit cyclists. The weeks had not flown by, but they had survived, would keep surviving. The vast supply of frozen casseroles, pickles, pre-serves and freeze-dried vegetable protein she'd accumulated in a frenzy before Christian was dwindling; she could see the back of her cupboards. Just in time, like magic, her new friends had supplied her with an apparently inexhaustible cornucopia of veg. Her savings were about to run out. Just in time, like magic, her new friends had found her a job — at a bike shop. She started tomorrow — today. It was just past midnight.

Time still wasn't something she could keep hold of, though after tonight, what the baby books called "the fourth trimester," that transitional space between life and the womb, would be technically over. People came and went at the Marble Bar, laughing, smoking, moving through linear timestreams she remembered the shape of but had forgotten how to occupy. She couldn't imagine having a drink right now; she was so tired it might kill her. She could sleep as soon as the bikes went by.

"Mama," Christian said, "I'm hungry." The voice was small and clear. She saw their lips move.

It was only natural: Children grew, they developed, learned, changed. "Milk?" said Aileen.

"Milk," said Christian with great confidence and finality. Aileen picked them up and bared her breast.

"Sing?" said Christian.

Aileen sang, not a lullaby or a nursery rhyme but the sample of a dub song she'd probably misheard at the block party, "I know you'll never let me down," over and over as Christian fastened onto her breast and sucked, hard. She should not imagine her personal individuality and essence being sucked out of her and into Christian, she knew it could only make this harder. She would not have nightmares about her own child. But to overcome dreams required willpower, resources that could be acquired only through sleep.

With Andrew to support her, Aileen had been a person in her own right, unique, even independent. Now Christian took precedence. She could have friends only because those friends pitied her and wanted to give of themselves to help her, and what did she have for them in return, except what Christian could give?

Except love.

Something hummed in her ear, a mosquito. She slapped at it. Christian slept, a three-month-old blob of fragile adorable- ness. Her smoothie sat in its pool of condensation on the sidewalk; she sucked. The door to the bar swung open; real music overwhelmed the chorus in her head as partiers spilled onto the sidewalk, some carrying bottles, lighting cigarettes, joints, the faint blue dot of a vaporizer.

A car approached, jostling and vibrating over the wrecked pavement, accompanied by a quiet, warning whine. Teardrop-shaped, silver, not a mark on it. Moving through intermittent pools of light from unbroken streetlamps like a fish through the deep. She bolted out of the rocker. This had happened before.

Voices raised on the opposite curb. Joints were extinguished, a few bottles were hucked away into the dark.

The spectral car slowed. The windows descended. There was no one inside. A bright light flashed three times; in its glare the partiers on the opposite curb were momentarily frozen in place. The window rose, the car accelerated away.

"Fucking drone!" Somebody threw a bottle, which exploded harmlessly on the street. This was followed by more cursing; a dustpan and broom were brought from the bar and the offender shoved out to clean up the hazard.

Down Holden through a wash of faint red moonlight and citylight came the first rider.

Aileen scooped Christian up and clutched them close.

The bike wasn't like any she'd seen. There might once have been tires; the metal rims cast sparks off the pavement. There were no brakes. The rider sat upright, relaxed, knees bowed out to the sides, barely touching the handlebars, giving Aileen the impression of a trick rider worn past the last thread, yet so comfortable in the saddle it was easier — for the moment, on this straight and level course — to keep on pedaling than to fall. A long coat indistinct in age, cut, or color fanned around them in tatters, echoing the shape and motion of the gnarled, colorless locks, so long they all but dragged on the road. The rider's face was in shadow.

Just behind the Elf, Virgil bent over the handlebars of Aileen's beautiful blue custom cruiser, riding hard, stood up on the pedals like he was climbing the Alps, but gaining no ground.

That the Elf existed at all, a being of flesh and blood who could be seen by moonlight, streetlight, wasn't something she could take in. That Virgil had been alive this whole past month, and had not shown his face at Aileen's door — not to bring some piece of trash to make her life easier, not to return her bike, not even to say hello — hurt. Not the way Andrew had, but too much like it. She couldn't let them go by. She opened her mouth to speak, to say *hey, it's me, remember me, what the fuck, that's my bike. Give it back. Come back.* She couldn't.

What *was* this? What was the Elf? Being outside of time — was it something they had in common? Existing a world apart from the experience of people who weren't mothers of infant children, who could pound beers at five minutes to midnight and throw them away into the street after half-smoked joints, and there would be no consequences, no one who depended on them for breath and sustenance would be placed in mortal peril. Was it the same? She needed to understand.

She stepped off the curb into the street.

Christian wriggled, dug toes into her breast. The riders approached.

They were moving so slow.

A fraction of a lifetime before the Elf would have had to swerve to avoid her, she lost her nerve and jumped back. The Elf did not swerve. The strange bike sailed by, scattering sparks at her feet. The streetlight revealed their face: fleetingly, somewhere between a laughing death's head and a ritual mask. Then they winked, wrinkles contracting like scales around a dark eye eminently alive, human.

It took forever for them to pass and be gone, then almost as long again for the main body of Night Rollers to appear, bringing music, slowing to wave and pop wheelies and groove in their saddles, encouraged by the Marble Bar crowd. Morris rode out in front — in third place, if it had been a race — far,

far behind the Elf and Virgil. She found Omar with the middle of the pack, but out at the edge, along the side he knew she would be watching from.

As Morris whizzed past the streetlight on a road bike three times fancier and higher-tech than her own, still probably only a tenth the cost of the autocar, she realized she ought to have had something for them, heirloom tomato slices, little cups of smoothie to hold out as to a Tour rider before a climb.

Her fingers closed around a fresh, unused burp cloth stuffed into her bra strap, reassuringly soft. She drew it out and held it aloft. Omar's fingers met hers as he took it. He threw it over one shoulder as he rode on.

Lunch packed in the diaper bag, Christian bundled to her chest, Aileen found Omar waiting at the curb, perched reading a fat fantasy novel on the trunk of a weathered, manual-drive sedan. He wore the burp cloth folded like a pocket square. She hugged him as tight as she dared around the baby. "*You* have a car?"

He shook his head, smiling behind his dark beard, looking only slightly the worse for having been up biking half the night. "My cousin's. You deserve a ride on your first day. And look!" He opened the passenger door with a flourish. "My nephew grew out of his car seat. She says you can keep it."

Aileen didn't have a car, was never going to have a car. But she'd turned up her nose at Virgil's industrial washtub bassinet, and what had that gotten her? Dew was already disappearing from the sidewalk in line with the sun. It would have been a long, hot wait at the bus stop.

Inside, it smelled of Thai food; toys littered the floor. "Air conditioning doesn't work," Omar said apologetically, "but the windows do!" The breeze was nice. The gas engine growled and exhaled unfiltered death and made the whole car vibrate in a way she imagined might have lulled her back to sleep if Christian hadn't hated the car seat. They screamed for three blocks until she couldn't take it anymore, Omar stopped, and she crammed in next to them and encouraged them to suck her pinky.

"So how does it feel?" asked Omar. "Sorry — going back to work, I mean. Are you ready?"

"No," she said, twisted awkwardly against the seat belt, Christian's still-toothless palate hot and insistent around her fingertip. "But I'm going. I think I slept three hours in a stretch? That's a record. I already wasn't working two months before Andrew left. I've had more time than I'm supposed to need."

"Nobody should be allowed to tell you how much time you need."

"Thanks," she said, awkwardly. "Without you guys, without Virgil, I don't know how we would have survived."

Omar deflected her gratitude with that now-familiar gesture, a hand to his temple. "You'd do it for us. I know you would. Look how hard you've been looking for Virgil."

"I'm not doing it for him, I'm doing it for me." Out the window, tiny houses with enormous garages crumbled, collapsed into weeds and reformed. Something told her Virgil wouldn't be here again and safe for a long time. She wasn't entirely sure anyone else in the world had ever known him, that he hadn't been some figment she dreamed up to feel less alone.

"Bullshit," said Omar gently. "And I'm not the only one who sees that. Reg asked about you."

She wasn't sure how to feel about that. "Was she riding? I didn't see her."

He shook his head. "At the after-party."

"What did she say?"

"'Squeeze that baby,'" he said in a fair impression of Reg's smoky baritone. "She thinks you could eat more."

She still had baby weight, but it had never been much. She changed the subject. "What about Virgil — did you see him?"

"Nope. And I didn't see the Elf, before you ask. I saw Morris, way out ahead of everybody, alone, like always. He says he saw them. Did you?"

"Both of them." She watched him try to come to terms with this.

"How — how did they look?"

Like they were racing to see who got to ride the pulse of the city, and Virgil was losing. Like they'd been frozen in time that way, forever, and the city itself, with all its ruin and renewal, its new influx of refugees, its aging robber barons and jaded revolutionaries, was the manifestation of that race.

But Omar had never seen the Elf. Didn't believe in them.

She hadn't, until last night.

He seemed to give up waiting for an answer.

The wind rushed. Christian's breath caught, calmed, caught again. It was only three miles, so close to flat she couldn't tell the difference, at least not in a car. Dedicated bike lane the whole way, as over most of the city, since it had been built for so many more cars. An easy, safe commute, if she could bike.

Omar braked suddenly as an autocar passed with its warning buzz, close and fast, beating a yellow light with perfect precision. "I hate those things."

Wheels on Fire was at 16th and Michigan, catty-corner across Roosevelt Park from Michigan Central Depot. Long abandoned, suddenly gutted and renovated into an upscale shopping and commercial center, the old train station hummed with activity. Autocars deposited and collected corporate suits and nuclear families from the colonnaded entryway;

a drone whizzed overhead. From the north side of Michigan Ave, across four lanes of car traffic, two bike lanes, and two parking lanes, Aileen felt as isolated from it as if it were a desert vision. Homeless people who used to sleep in Roosevelt Park now did so on the opposite sidewalk, evidenced by nests of sleeping bags against the walls below the storefronts. Chicory blossomed blue and robust from cracks in the brick.

At the curb, Omar tried gamely but failed to help get Christian out of the car seat and re-bundled to her chest. "Sorry I can't pick you up — my cousin needs the car, and anyway my shift doesn't end til two a.m." He promised the car seat would be waiting in the alley behind Holden and Trumbull when she got home. "Good luck," he said.

"Get in here," said Rosaria from the open door, "and let's see what you can do."

In her previous life, Aileen had spent two years getting paid, basically, to make the same microgreen salad over and over, dressed with a reduction of sour cherries and Belgian ale vinegar, wild mustard flower garnish applied with tweezers, for people like those debarking from their private autocars to shop at the mirage across the street. But no restaurant wanted kitchen staff with a three-month-old strapped between their breasts. She'd known that a year ago, when her plan had been — nothing like this. Mothering full-time at least until Christian was ready for day care. Now she couldn't even think that far ahead.

She knew she could fix a bike. She figured she could sell them. With Morris's recommendation, the owner had believed it, too. She needed the work. She needed the money.

Inside, it wasn't cool, just dark. A fan blew deep and throaty from somewhere back in the warehouse space.

Rosaria had red lips and lacquer-black hair that resculpted itself as she moved, which she did with a clipped, fearsome energy. She made only the tokenest of efforts to conceal the black bike shorts she wore under a loud, short dress. Her legs were amazing. "I'm hiring you because of her," she said, nodding to Christian, who gazed at a fixed point to the left of the mural, too far away for them to see, and blew spit bubbles.

"They," corrected Aileen, *almost* without hesitation, and allowed herself a little bit of pride.

A crease appeared between Rosaria's black brows, and she moved on without pausing, leading Aileen between rows of refurbished, no-frills cruisers and commuter bikes, fixies, fat tire bikes, high-end racing bikes. All the way to the very back corner of the showroom, past the workshop, past kid trailers and a couple of recumbent trikes. "I don't care that you're not from here," said Rosaria. "As long as you intend to stay. I want that baby to grow up a part of this place. We need people to grow up here and love it, fight for it, make it worth living in. We need people not to run away."

"Okay," said Aileen, who had nowhere to run to.

"You know what this is?"

A beautiful, eggshell-gray bruiser of an e-assist cargo bike slumbered under a light haze of dust. Aileen nodded, trying not to drool. It was groceries. Laundry. Trips to the doctor. To the river. To work and back. To school and back, when it came to that. It was a future.

Rosaria made a rude gesture. "As far as I'm concerned, a bike that costs as much as a car defeats the purpose. Maybe they'd mean something if they were mass-produced instead of custom. I keep one around in case some industry asshole walks in one day and wants to keep my business open for a year singlehanded. But — just look. The e-assist goes up to 30 kph, battery only lasts for 20 minutes of use, but you're not meant to rely on it. Charges in something like two hours from an ordinary wall plug. Regenerative braking on all three wheels. LED headlights, taillights. Some people think it's cheating. I used to think so. But I've tried it — it's kind of freeing. It lets you compete with cars, in short bursts anyway, which is all you need. It feels — weirdly safe. Test ride it, you'll see. You'd think it's heavy, but it's not." She wrapped one hand around a place where the dust had already been disturbed and hefted the whole thing off the floor. "And look, here." The mounting places for a car seat.

"Why are you showing me this?"

She shrugged. "You'd have noticed anyway. And I want you to have something to want."

"Keeping myself and my baby alive isn't enough?"

"No, it isn't. People need hope."

Apparently they'd all been conspiring against her. For her.

Rosaria put her to work ("for now, as a trial") tuning up the huge collection of decrepit bikes from the back warehouse. There were hundreds, some rusted beyond repair, some without seats or brakes or wheels, some just in need of oil and adjustment. "People donate them. Sometimes I pick one up from the side of the road, if it's clear nobody's coming back for it and it isn't already turning to dirt. They don't need to be beautiful, just rideable, safe. Mostly I give them away, to churches, community groups. The idea is to get them to people who'll use them."

One bike near the back looked like her blue racer, but two generations older, the chrome all brown with rust, brakepads and tires rotting away. "You should sell that one for scrap," she told Rosaria. "They don't make those kind of fittings anymore."

Each of these bikes had a story, each had belonged to a person, a series of people, who had grown up or moved on or given up or died. People from the block party. People like those buzzing in and out of the mall. People she'd never met and couldn't imagine. Aileen picked out a smallish kids' bike, and with gritted teeth managed to heave it up onto a repair stand. The books said it was okay to start lifting things again; she had to start somewhere. She set to work scouring rust from the gears with steel wool and a spray bottle of solvent, careful to keep Christian out of the line of fire.

The nice thing about having a baby strapped to your chest, their head was always available for kissing. "Thank you," she told them quietly. "You are the hardest and worst and also the best thing that's ever happened to me."

Rosaria helped a few customers, not many considering the never-ending flow of traffic across the street. Was the whole city like this? Had it always been? A divide, a chasm: the kind of people who ever bothered to visit the far side of the street and the kind who didn't, the kind who left bikes abandoned to be devoured by time and the kind who took them home and fixed them. Aileen could feel the energy pent up in Rosaria, the way she let it out only under tight control, and wished for some small part of that energy for her own. At the end of the day, her shoulders and forearms and lower back ached, from the work and from carrying the baby, and her fingers stung from a combination of grease, rust, oil, and solvents. She just wanted to fall over; first she had to wait for the bus. "I'd offer you a ride home, but ..." Rosaria trailed off with something close to a smirk, pulling a pink helmet from under the counter.

From the bus stop in the lengthening light of afternoon, the shadow of the train depot marching past her, Aileen pined for the cargo bike, lurking immaculate and mocking at the back of the showroom.

She was never going to be able to afford it. Not for years. Not until it became moot. She'd done the math. She said so to Omar at Marble Bar on Friday night, spending a little off the top of her first meager paycheck in months. "I know that's why you got me the car seat, and I appreciate it, I do. But Christian would practically be able to ride a bike themself by the time I saved enough. To say nothing about other things I should be saving for, like college. Sorry, that's a joke, who saves for college?" She laughed, a little giddily. Growing up, she'd always had money. The world was changed forever.

"That's a *virgin* margarita, you know," said Omar. "Try not to make me look bad, there's some people I want you to meet." Musicians, a punk band — their set started later, long after Aileen and Christian would be in bed. They smiled and shook hands and made adoring sounds at the baby and started to offer her a seat, and she started to politely refuse because she was exhausted.

"Noreen, tell her what you told me. About Virgil."

Noreen was the drummer. He was young, skinny, with wild hair, thrift store clothes, and a comically large can of beer in front of him, like the rest of them. He looked lost. "He's my dad. I mean — I haven't seen him in a year, I wasn't sure he was still around. He and my mom never lived together. Not that I can remember. But yeah. Tall guy, big hands, kind of shaky, track suit, loves babies?"

Aileen sat down.

Virgil had been a character in her imagination now for months. To find outside corroboration for his existence ... of course, his house was still there down the street. But it wasn't his house. And she could talk to his neighbors, Frank and Gladys. She just hadn't. She didn't know why she was surprised. People needed people; they didn't exist in a vacuum.

The band was staring at her. Christian lolled their head around in their wrap, drooling, trying, she assumed, to take in everything at once.

"Virgil took care of Aileen for awhile after Christian was born," Omar prompted. "Then he kind of ... disappeared?" He refreshed her margarita.

"He didn't disappear," she said after a breath and a long, desperate sip. "I know where he is, I just don't know if he's coming back."

"Can I hold her?" asked the bass player.

"Them," said Aileen. "I want to let Christian decide who they are. But — yes, sure, if you want to."

She didn't know them. She didn't have to tell them. But Noreen deserved to know.

So she told the story in a rush, watched them squirm and not know how to react and question her sanity and her fitness to take care of a child. They weren't that much younger than she was, but it was like looking at them from the other side of a desert she'd just dragged herself across.

The bar was filling up; Omar couldn't hang around, but she caught his sympathetic glance. The late light was turning orange beyond the one smoky window.

"I'm sorry," she said, shaking herself, "but we really need to go eat something and sleep until time starts over." Christian was fine, lighting up everyone who laid eyes on them, smelling only faintly of spit-up and spoiled breast milk, but Aileen was finished. She collected them from the lead singer's arms, who looked relieved. *You have no idea,* she wanted to say.

Noreen got up hastily. "Can I walk you home?"

He was so young. She ran fingertips over the puffy skin beneath her eyes. "I live across the street. But thank you," she added at his disappointed look, and then realized that wasn't going to be enough.

❦

Noreen came by at eleven the next morning, underslept and awkward. She made him drink a glass of water while she changed Christian and dressed them. He talked about the show, the small but appreciative crowd, the free drinks. He laughed at himself; she felt a little more comfortable. He commented on Christian's bassinet. When he found out where it came from, he told her how Virgil had helped scavenge pieces for his drum kit, and she felt more comfortable still.

"Was he ... a good father? I mean, were you ever mad that he wasn't around more?"

"Yeah, no. I get that a lot, you know, like I'm either supposed to hate him for leaving or hate my mom and think he's some kind of hero. I guess I felt that way a long time ago. But that's who he is — kind of a mess, but not a bad guy. He gets hung up on an idea. You can't get him to talk about anything else hardly. And then it falls through, and he's down, really down for awhile. And then he gets caught on something else."

They walked together down Marquette to Frank and Gladys's. Aileen climbed their porch, wary of splinters, knocked, waited, squinting, sweating, and asked Gladys to hold Christian for ten minutes while they went across the street.

"*This* is where he was living?"

The lawn, what remained of it, was dead, the yard more forest than lawn. The CONDEMNED notice taped behind the screen door was weathered to unreadability. There were enough around — and Andrew had been curious enough when they'd arrived from the East Coast — that she remembered what they said: that it was both illegal and a very bad idea healthwise to trespass on this property, that it had been declared unsafe for human habitation by some government entity whose initials she forgot, and also that it had been repossessed by whatever bank. The front windows had long ago been replaced with glass block, the rest with plywood. Someone had held out a while before giving up: glass block wasn't cheap, but you couldn't smash it. She wondered where the owners were now, what had been the tipping point, what would it take to make them come back. What the rest of the world would have to look like first.

She thought about those abandoned bikes decomposing into sidewalk, Rosita rescuing and resuscitating them, sending them out again into the world. Was there an equivalent for houses? Was this it? Chicory growing from cracks, mulberry roots pushing them wider — how many years before every house like this collapsed into a forested mound? For the next colonizers — same as the first — to build their forts on.

The door was unlocked.

Across the street, Frank and Gladys had retreated with Christian back into their house; she had to hope it was safer than in Virgil's. She looked at Noreen, trying to read him. "Are we —" Really doing this, she wanted to ask. He'd already stepped past her.

Inside it was airless and oppressive: stale takeout grease, burned wiring, dust and beer. She covered her mouth. Her eyes struggled to adjust. A gash in the plaster, torn at shin-level where someone had stolen the hot water pipes, exposed wooden ribs and something that looked like animal hair. Noreen stood at the end of the hallway, looking at a photograph on the fridge.

"That's him. That's — us, I guess."

She joined him. Every inch of floor creaked. A couple and a baby in front of a brick church with white columns — not the one from her dreams? Virgil, it was Virgil in a ruffled white bell-bottom tuxedo and smoked glasses.

"You've never seen this?"

"He never brought me over to his place. Now I know why."

She wasn't about to open the fridge. On the counter by the sink sat a few empty water jugs, a few full. On the wall, an auto repair company calendar marked up with "WORK," "CLASS," "LIBRARY," "Y," "AA." Every Sunday for weeks said "AILEEN." She flipped back. A Saturday, more than a month ago: "ROLL."

Noreen pulled out a chair and sat down at the kitchen table, folded his hands on the formica next to some pens and pencils, a mug, a pile of mail, a battery-powered boom box, a pile of library books. He didn't look at any of it, instead stared down the hallway at the door, his mouth going through a series of tight contortions. A drop of sweat fell from his chin.

"We don't have to stay," she said gently.

"Yeah. Okay," said Noreen, subdued.

She took the books. *The Cycling City, Iron Riders, The Great Migration, Major Taylor, The Origin of the Urban Crisis,* and *Manabozho Legends.* They were probably overdue.

They left, floorboards protesting with every step.

She didn't feel right again until she had Christian in her arms.

"Any time, dear," said Gladys, a cold wind of air condition-ing blowing from behind her. "Seriously. You know where to find us. Your little boy is such a delight."

"I'll, uh, I'll see you," said Noreen.

Just when she finally needed him, when she had questions, im-portant questions, Virgil's shade would not appear. She sat in the rocker while Christian slept, in the full, deep scrutiny of the fan, Virgil's overdue library books spread out in front of her on the floor, looking out at the day turning orange along Holden, waiting for the long hands of the almost-dead locust tree's shadow on the corner of Sterling to reach as far as her doorstep, waiting for sleep and dreams that wouldn't come, thinking of all the rooms in Virgil's house she hadn't been into, the bedrooms, the bathroom, the basement, whether any of them had windows that worked, if anything at all was left of the people who owned that house, where he went to the bath-room, if not the bathroom, where he slept, why. *Why are you doing this? What did you think it would achieve — or was it just some crazy notion — and even if it was, how could you forget about us?*

She'd been on his calendar, the very next day.

When she slept, she was visited not by Virgil's shade but Christian's, their future self, the little towheaded boy-girl she had biked past in another dream, talking to some older kids sitting on a curb in some other neighborhood she'd never be able to see until she could bike past it, talking matter-of-factly about a life she couldn't access, a life formulated on weekend block parties and summers off from school and a stable, patient, trusting, absent-only-because-working mother.

She woke and she wanted that. All of it except her absence.

"So make it happen," she told herself, telling Christian.

"So make one yourself," Rosaria told her first thing Monday morning, knuckles placed on her hips so her already-greasy fingers wouldn't smudge her rainbow dress, cocking her head appraisingly at the beautiful, sleek cargo bike, flushed from shadow at the back of the shop like a great elk from a thicket when she flicked on the lights. "Do it cheap and ugly. You don't need battery backup — look at your calves! Do it heavy. You don't need titanium, use steel. I'm not set up for metalwork yet, but it wouldn't be that hard. Get two bikes — take whatever you want from the warehouse, I don't care, we'll get more. Chop one of them in half, fuse two rear forks to fit two wheels on an axle. Use the rest to build the cargo bed. Find help. This is Detroit. You can't throw a piece of rotten brick without hitting an unemployed machine shop worker. It's about finding one who's not an asshole."

She found one, asking around at the block party that weekend: Frank, Gladys's husband, Virgil's neighbor, who'd been forcibly retired from Ford he wouldn't say how long ago and now divided his time between doctor's appointments, sipping vape tobacco on his porch and annoying his wife. "I was so proud of him for quitting cigarettes," said Gladys.

"Just don't get him started about unions," warned Reg. "Don't get me started," and she swigged long from a beer and went off looking for a mic.

Aileen insisted on paying for his time, after they couldn't come to an agreement where she paid him in smoothies and microgreen salads. He didn't own a bike, hadn't ridden a bike since he was twelve. She bought him a membership to a maker co-op in Hazel Park. She wasn't allowed to bring Christian inside, even in protective ear and eyewear, but the roar of machine saws was more than audible through the walls while she waited by the loading dock, sipping water, clinging to the building's shade, reading *The Origin of the Urban Crisis*, singing "Wayfaring Stranger" to Christian over and over.

"Bunch of young guys treat us like we're made of glass," he said, when he came out an hour later, laughing with a fellow grizzled, tattooed ex-UAW retiree, "but we'll manage."

She took Frank to Rosaria's warehouse looking for materials, but he said there was nothing he could work with — it was all cheap aluminum or rusted or weathered too thin. "Get what you pay for," he said.

Everything took ten times longer than it should, even after some of it started to feel routine. She was working eight hours, sleeping twelve, actually sleeping six, which left a precious four hours in a day to wait for buses, cook, do laundry, and figure out how to build a cargo bike out of nothing. After a few weeks, the soreness of wearing Christian everywhere faded. She couldn't really even smell the spit-up anymore. Her hands stopped stinging from the work just in time for Rosaria to believe she was serious and move her to the front of the store. But the buses, the waiting on corners — she hadn't seen Andrew again, she didn't know if it had been Andrew, but it made her feel isolated and alone, and there was no remedy for it, and there wouldn't be. Even when she'd made a cargo bike, she wouldn't be able to ride it. There was nothing but waiting. So she waited. And while she waited, she quested.

She took Virgil's books reluctantly back to the big library in Midtown after reading as much of them as she could bear, paid the fines, and checked out others. She tried to catch up to Frank a little, in hopes of understanding some of what he was saying about materials and machines. She tried to understand what had made him this way — and Virgil, Noreen, Omar, Morris, Gladys, Rosaria, and Reg. What had made this city.

She found confirmation of some of Reg's story about Antoine de la Mothe Cadillac, the "founder" of Detroit, "one of the worst scoundrels ever to set foot in New France." She came across a fragment about two French priests who'd smashed a stone effigy they took for a golden calf at the mouth of the Detroit River in 1610. She read about the Three Fires Confederacy of the Ojibwe, Odawa, and Potawatomi, founded a thousand years before the Treaty of 1807 ceded the Straits of Detroit to the United States. She learned parts of Detroit had once been paved in wood, in a space of ten or twenty years before the automobile had taken hold, when the bicycle dominated the city, and that among those who had introduced cycling here were the veterans of a Black bicycle cavalry regiment in the Civil War, the Iron Riders. She read a book of children's stories in which the Elf figured as a kind of gremlin plaguing the burgeoning auto industry at the turn of the century. She found a picture of the church Virgil had gotten married in — the Shrine of the Black Madonna — in a newspaper article about the '67 Rebellion. She didn't have the focus or attention to read deeply, she was too tired, and there was a baby drooling, babbling, occasionally shitting and shrieking between her breasts.

She bought a bike online, a heavy, steel-framed mountain bike at least twenty years old, in perfect condition, as if it had spent that time pursuing the Elf through some empty limbo while everything else aged around it. She and Christian took a bus up Livernois to Sherwood Forest on a Sunday to collect it from an old woman's garage half-decomposed to loam. Aileen sat with her under a huge, sick oak in the barren backyard of a brick Victorian, listening to her talk about her son, who had helped her list the bike, who wouldn't be needing it anymore because he'd moved away, the opposite of Aileen except that he still had a mom to come back to and a home to come back to her in. She paid twenty dollars above the asking price because she could. Walking the bike with Christian strapped to her chest through deeply shaded neighborhoods of long-ago wealth slowly rising from and falling into ruin felt at first ridiculously indulgent, as if she could throw a leg over and take off anytime she wanted, then impatient and incredibly slow, then exhausted, and finally stupid. She wouldn't be able to ride it for months. The hard plastic saddle hurt just to look at. The sharp pedal dug into her leg every pace and a half, until she was leaning on it like a crutch, limping.

She went back out to Livernois and waited for the bus.

She fought the heavy bike upstairs, then lay curled around Christian on her bed for an hour, crying, thinking about lost home, until Morris and Omar came over for dinner. Morris held Christian and Omar held her, and she indulgently allowed herself to hold him back like a lover, her hand on the firm muscle of his back, and Omar indulgently let her. She tried to explain how you couldn't go home even if you wanted to, nobody could, how things changed for everyone, you couldn't be young again, nobody would ever mother you like you'd been mothered. And they nodded and said solemnly that it was true. Omar told about having to mother his parents, hold their hands through fears of hate and deportation he'd never known as a kid because they'd sheltered him. And Morris, with only a little prompting from Omar, told how he'd taken the bus home in the spring, to that lonely, impoverished paradise above the Lake that made him hurt with beauty and miss his garden plot surrounded by ugly brick projects and friends. And they made dinner. They were her family and her home now, and she told them so with more tears, this time of gratitude and relief.

She gave up the quest for a little while.

Then Morris found her another bike like the first, the same make and model, a few years older, almost as well-preserved. She saw him out the bus window coming home from Wheels on Fire — he'd rigged it so he could pull it behind him on his own bike, a ghost bike with an absent rider. She knocked on the window, and he waved, then pumped harder, putting on speed, outpacing the bus when it stopped at a light.

He was waiting when they got home, flushed and smiling, his great shoulders heaving. He even carried the bike upstairs.

The two bikes together, leaning end to end against the kitchen island, were so beautiful she almost didn't want to touch them. Suddenly she could see it, see them taken apart and re-fused, made one. And then it was happening.

46

Omar had to talk her into actually going to see it being done. She wasn't allowed into the machine shop with Frank to see the sparks fly — not if she wanted to take Christian. And without Christian, what was the point?

"You are," said Omar gently, and arranged for Gladys to take Christian for an afternoon.

She wore protective earmuffs and wraparound plastic glasses and stood with arms protectively folded around her belly in an artificially cold, vibrating warehouse space full of hammering, sawing, laughter, lasers, and old machines burnished with the oils of human hands, the floor worn with track marks, the cavernous ceiling strung with harsh lights, watching the two bikes divided and re-formed by a molten knife. When she came out again into the day, her jaw hurt from clenching and her ears rung, and she wanted very much to hold onto something green. Or Christian.

Frank delivered the finished bike a week later. She shook his callused hand, hugged him, and promised to bring Christian by for lunch on Sunday. She insisted on bringing salad only she and Gladys would eat.

And then there was nothing left but to run shifter and brake cables, order the hardware to allow the cargo bed to accept the car seat, and install it, and a bell, head- and tail-lights, a wide, cushioned seat, and look into baby bike helmets, and look around the alley behind her building for a loop of iron to lock it to so she wouldn't have to haul the bike up and down-stairs.

After lunch with Frank and Gladys, she went across the street to Virgil's for the calendar, in and out as quickly and carefully as she could, opening no doors, trying hard not to breathe.

She hung the calendar on her own apartment door when she got home, flipped ahead past pictures of elk drinking from streams and icebound waterfalls in the pristine, inaccessible peninsulas of the North, from somewhere among which she knew Morris's family had come. Not that she understood what that meant.

The last Saturday in October, two days past Christian's half-birthday, she marked in block letters like Virgil's: "ROLL."

It was Hallowe'en.

3

August's heat lingered through September, though the shadows of buildings and trees across Trumbull grew longer, and pumpkins and acorn squash began to come into season at Eastern Market. The bike waited in the back alley, trembling with life and potential, impossibly patient. She couldn't help stopping to visit on the way to the bus stop in the morning, sometimes again despite exhaustion on the way home. She'd removed the cushy seat and the front wheel and brought them upstairs, and the lock that secured it to the fire escape cost more than either bike, keeping her from taking it for a spin before it was time. She admired the way the dusky purples and greens of the bikes it had been made from ran together at the seams. She lined her eye up with the rear axle to reassure herself the rear wheels were perfectly aligned. She squeezed the brakes to test the tension. She gently, very gently, rang the bell.

By this time Rosaria had Aileen working sales, and she could watch the easy, comfortable part of humanity to which she'd once belonged float past, in and out of the depot mall, laughing, their eyes concealed, leaving compostable containers of barbecue leftovers with the homeless people on the sidewalks, talking loudly about things that did not fucking matter. Some of them even came into the shop, and she told them about bikes, calmly and enthusiastically, while they cooed over Christian and misgendered them sometimes even after she corrected them.

The changes in Christian were gradual, hardly noticeable until she took a step back and let herself be shocked. They were holding their head up under their own power, then sitting up, rolling on the floor laughing like crazy, then they were crawling. Soon, soon, the time would come when she couldn't strap them to her chest and go to work, and her whole life would change again.

They hadn't spoken a word, only babbled.

She kept reading, though it was still hard to focus or to feel at any time truly, completely awake. She read that no Native claim to this land was recognized until the year she was born, and thought she understood better Morris's moments of cold impenetrability. She read about innovation, industrialization, "the arsenal of democracy," robber barons, housing discrimination, ghettoization, rioting, looting, white flight, urban blight, and gentrification. She read about Shawn Johns, a four-year-old shot to death with a fifty caliber machine gun during the Rebellion by a police officer terrified of a sniper who turned out not to exist, and she cried bitterly for Shawn's mother, who she learned had died in April, the week Christian was born.

She went to block parties. She listened to Reg perform and tell stories and didn't ask her, or Frank or Gladys, what it had been like. Reg had been a child, only a little older than Shawn Johns.

Noreen came, and she thought she remembered having seen him there before, though his band never played. "Not the right kind of music," he said ruefully. He pointed out his mother, a plump, smiling woman in bright colors, talking animatedly. Aileen saw her talking to Virgil like that, Virgil talking back. *Easy. Like a dough on the rise.*

"I'd honestly rather you didn't," said Noreen, to Aileen's guilty relief, before she could ask. "I don't think she wants to be reminded."

She daydreamed of that place she began to believe she had once visited in dreams, the Elf's limbo, of Virgil clinging desperately to its outer rim, the city changing around him the way Christian had, in an unfathomable rush. Inside it, you were suspended, safe, and outside it, everyone thought of you with hope and loss, or not at all.

Morris and Omar came to dinner again. Omar lay sprawled on the floor with Christian, tickling them, reciting Omar Khayyam and Miz Corona lyrics, lifting them up on chubby legs and encouraging them to dance. Morris expertly processed squash for pickling and talked about the harvest, about composting and contaminated soil, about reverse-engineering and adapting ancient foodways with and without help from survivors.

Aileen asked, carefully, if his family grew food.

"My dad was a CNC operator. My mom tried. Then she moved to Chicago after they split. She had a rosemary plant in the window, last I was there."

"My mom grows eggplants," Omar volunteered into the quiet.

They hadn't been talking to each other much, except about Christian and Aileen. It was Morris and Omar; there was no one she felt safer with, now that Virgil was gone. Still, sometimes, there was this wall.

"September Night Roll is coming up," she tried instead. "I was thinking I might ride."

The click of Morris's knife work paused. The fan thrummed; hot air cycled through the room. "Ah!" said Christian loudly into the white noise, waving their hands.

"I know, baby," said Aileen.

"Is it safe for you?" asked Omar. "I mean ..."

"It would hurt, I'm pretty sure," she said. "But I've got to start sometime."

"Would you take Christian?"

"No, they're too young. They need to be at least six months, it has to do with skull development. I'm not going to risk it. They can wait for October."

"But you'd risk yourself." The disapproval was plain in his voice.

"She gets to decide that," Morris cut in, before Aileen could respond.

"Thank you," she told Morris. She'd been expecting this. Omar was protective. And she appreciated that, up to a point. Morris was — an individualist? — in ways that weren't always to anyone's benefit. He needed Omar taking care of him as much as she did. "And I'm being careful with myself too," she told them. "I don't need to do the whole ride. Especially since I'd have to ask someone to watch Christian. I just don't want Hallowe'en to be my first time, you know? I thought I'd try standing on the pedals. So I don't have to sit down."

"I'll ride with you," said Omar. "In case you need to quit early, you'll need somebody to help you get home. That thing's so big, you're not going to be able to hop on a bus anymore."

"Actually," said Aileen, "I was going to ask you to stay with Christian. I can't ask Gladys to stay up that late."

Omar frowned.

"But you're right — it would be good to have someone to go with me, too. I could walk the bike home, but —"

"I can," Morris volunteered, looking startled.

"Thank you," said Aileen.

"Why leave it for the Roll?" said Morris. "You can practice anytime."

"I will," she said. "And if it hurts too much, I'll wait. Okay?"

"I think they need to be changed," said Omar. "Why don't I do it."

The cargo bike's seat and front wheel hung clipped to the wall where her old blue bike used to go. Getting them down, bringing them downstairs and around to the back alley, Morris and Omar at her heels, Christian on her shoulder — it felt huge, monumental. She savored it, lingering over the tire pressure, adjusting the saddle. The sun was noticeably lower in the sky than at this hour a month ago, the light a deeper gold.

The moment she stood up on the pedals, she knew the doctors' warnings had nothing to do with the breadth or comfort of the seat. It was the exertion, the physical effort of moving muscles recently torn, still healing. She was slowing her recovery with every revolution.

But it was glorious. The wind in her face, the movement, the world rolling by.

She kept going as long as she dared. Right on Stirling past the locust trees, all the way north to Grand Boulevard, a glance across the broad street at the hospital where Christian had been born, a long look at the art deco spire of the Fisher Building rising from the haze-shimmering horizon, then back down Trumbull, past acres of vacant lots scattered with black walnut and cottonwood, past Virgil's house, Gladys and Frank's, and back to the end of the alley, where there was no place to go but upstairs again.

Almost a mile. She put on a good face for Morris and Omar, because she couldn't let them stop her. The face she showed Christian, though, was real.

Thinking of Omar, who wanted her to think of herself, she took care of herself every other way she could. She ate well, took her vitamins, experimented with sitz baths and homemade herbal oils and extracts that made the loft smell like a witch's kitchen, drew flies and wandering cats, who left disappointed. She took Christian to the doctor for their vaccinations and checkups and tried not to feel insulted by the questions.

Reg the Redeemer came by unexpectedly Saturday afternoon, a week before the full moon, accompanied by a pair of hangers-on — hypewomen? She took the rocking chair, the other two ended up lounging awkwardly by the windows, the first time Aileen had felt embarrassed about not owning a couch. Andrew had always been moving, or else lying flat on the floor.

"Okay if we smoke this?"

"Uh." Christian was sleeping. "Just —" She dragged the fan around to point out the window. "You guys want some blueberry smoothie?"

Reg rocked, her stubby gray braids moving almost imperceptibly in the fan. She waved a deflecting hand.

Aileen, nursing her smoothie, now mostly watery ice, considered a kitchen stool, sat on a pillow on the rug instead. She waited, unsure what was expected of her.

"You all right? Need anything?"

"I'm okay," she said. Meaning it. It had been a long time coming. She didn't know how to say so to Reg. "Tired, but there's not much helping that. I could stand to do a load of laundry or three."

She meant it as a joke. But the hangers-on passed the joint, leaving it with Reg, and before Aileen realized what was happening, they'd filled two baskets and disappeared downstairs.

Reg rocked all the way back and breathed smoke, her voice deep. "Omar thinks you need somebody to talk to. A mother. Said he thought about his cousin, but that would be weird since you never met her."

Not as weird as this. "I didn't know you had kids."

"Two. They're in college — one at Detroit Mercy, one at Oakland. Does that surprise you?"

Aileen felt her cheeks flush, remembering Reg's words from that first block party. *Got to learn to live with them somehow.* She followed Reg's gaze among the library books scattered with the baby things and thought of what they represented, an outsider trying to understand. There were things she never would. Until she raised a child here? "He thinks I'm moving too fast. That I'm not taking care of myself. But I am. I just can't wait anymore. I tried staying isolated from everything. Omar's the one who pulled me out of that. Now I'm finally about to be able to do something on my own, and I feel like I might explode. I mean if I don't collapse first."

Reg laughed. "Sounds like you could use some of this."

Aileen shook her head. "Don't think I'm not tempted." She wasn't. She'd had enough hallucinations. "I'd be asleep before I could exhale."

"Listen," said Reg, gesturing with it, faint trails dissipating. "I had my first baby when I was nineteen. I know it changes you. How you see the world. It took me a little while, but I didn't let it stop me. Everybody's got to make their own choices how to find that balance. And people without kids can be ... rough."

"Sometimes I wonder how anybody can do this," said Aileen.

"Raise babies? You ask me, they can't. Nobody knows what they're doing, they just do it, and it comes out all right. Or it doesn't. I don't want you thinking I'm any kind of great mother. In my experience, all the great mothers are dead. I'm what you get."

Aileen's mother was dead. She hadn't been a great mother. Aileen could have really used her help. "So you're saying whatever I do is ... fine." She laughed, a little hysterically.

Reg shrugged and hit the joint again. "Sorry," she said. "This isn't exactly my area of expertise." In the bassinet in the other room, Christian started to cry.

Aileen took a breath, felt it catch. "I don't suppose you could rephrase that in the form of a hug?"

The rocker creaked as Reg got up. She put out the joint with a fingertip and hid it away somewhere Aileen didn't see.

She was small, smaller than Aileen, smaller than her presence and the mic made her out to be, but her embrace was strong. She was soft and hard in what seemed like the wrong places. Aileen pulled back momentarily — but it didn't matter. The dank smell reminded her, inevitably, of Andrew. Christian's cries got louder, more panicked, as if they were suddenly sure no one was coming.

"I should go get the baby," said Aileen.

"Right," said Reg, and let go.

55

Michael J. DeLuca

She waited while Aileen changed and fed them, while Aileen murmured gentle, incoherent words about blackness, whiteness, the future, the past, how you were expected to make head or tail of them and decide, until Christian quieted and found their latch and drank. Reg waited some more, awkwardly. She accepted Aileen's offer of the half glass of smoothie that was left and didn't blink when Aileen tried to joke it was okay if she needed to spike it. From the floor, Reg picked up a book of essays about the Rebellion.

It was quiet a little while.

Andrew had once sat with his arms around her on the musty couch in their old apartment, the little glass pipe smoldering on the table in front of them, talking excitedly about their cross-country journey, getting Aileen excited too. He'd spent weeks selling off their shit online, reducing them to what would fit in his little manual-transmission sedan somehow survived from the early aughts. He'd driven the whole way from the coast in one go, the fourteen hours or whatever it took, stopping only to pee and scrounge vegetable fuel, their bikes on the back, windows open a crack, the smoke draining into the slipstream. In the last hour, the roads had turned to pitted ruin. The first sign it would not be as he'd foretold.

Those memories began to seem less than real, experiences she'd lived but could no longer access as her own, like a historian's retelling of a riot.

The hangers-on returned with the wash, and Reg seemed to shake something off, or take it on again: her mantle of authority. "I hear you're riding on Saturday. Good for you. Like I said, nobody's asking you to be a great mother. You're already a mother. You get to be a person too. Just — don't ask for too much. Omar thinks — well, that doesn't matter." She threw down the book she'd been flipping through with a bang that startled the hangers-on and the baby. She re-sparked the roach, took a long, shallow hit from it pinched at the tips of her fingers. "I'm trying to tell you that story about the Elf is just one version. Not even mine. Not — you know, true. You

56

understand? There was no Detroit Elf, not then, not in sixty-seven, there's no Elf now. All this history you're reading? Anybody's idea what happened is as true as anybody else's, for all it matters. Virgil's maybe least of all."

Heat. Sweat rolled from her hairline and down her spine, the first Aileen felt she had earned in five months: fast-moving blood elicited by her own heart pumping. There was burning, in her lower back and thighs as well as her groin.

Water, in a flask, icy cold, with an herby, deep-green splash of nettle tonic, sloshed in its cage between her ankles if she needed it. She was pedaling too hard to reach.

Stones. Michigan Ave's mix of cobblestones and crumbling tar retained the sun's warmth and smelled bituminous and rich as Black Bottom earth in the night, and she could not for the life of her, for all the fairy lights strung on the bikes of all the riders, the pedal-powered headlights, the streetlights, see the next pothole when it came. Though it jarred, she didn't fall, because her bike was a trike. And she triumphed in it.

Wind, artificial, made by her movement, carried alcohol, exhaust, raw gasoline, and the signature sulfurous salt clouds of the Detroit underground billowing from the grates.

When it was over and she sat gasping on the curb, pulse roaring, head between her knees trying not to throw up from the exertion, the sensations came back to her, overwhelming, and for long moments she could not think past them even to wonder why now or where they had been, where she had been. She thought of Christian exerting their muscles for the first time, learning to sit up, to crawl — did it feel like this? Learning to walk, what was that like? Did falling hurt? No, no, babies had jelly bones, it wasn't the same.

She thought of giving birth.

When the pain of exertion subsided enough to let her reach for the flask, wrench it free and drink, she became aware of the city, the brick and concrete and the empty space, the thin traffic, the lights of downtown low in the east like the threat of dawn. The Night Rollers on their bikes were gone.

It had all been different. The buildings, the street signs, even the names had changed. Two miles — she'd only meant to ride two miles. This was Rosa Parks and Michigan — 13th Street, the sign had said, but there was no 13th Street. They had to have come across the highway overpass at 14th. She couldn't remember.

Where was Morris? He'd been behind her. Right behind her, for awhile. She'd passed him. On her heavy, klunky cargo trike, she'd passed Morris bent low over the handlebars of his custom, stripped-down, titanium racing bike. She'd observed, from a place of detachment, his astonishment and frustration, the sunflowers flexing and relaxing on his calves. He hadn't stopped for her. The plan had been for him to stop, to help her get home. She was alone. She couldn't ride any further. She couldn't. Where was Christian? Safe with Omar.

She drank, emptying her flask, gulping. She breathed and held onto her knees.

She got out her phone to call him. As she lifted it to her ear, an automated car approached along Michigan, teardrop-shaped. It slowed and pulled to a stop beside her, gleaming under the streetlight, humming in unobtrusive electric supremacy. A rear door opened. If she hadn't been utterly, physically spent she might have jumped out of her own skin. A man in a suit got out, a phone to his own ear. He beckoned.

"Hello? Aileen?" said Omar's voice on her phone. "We're fine — Christian's fine. What happened? Where are you?"

Billy Beaurein's office was cold, full of sleek, unidentifiable machines, the most recognizable of which were a wheelchair in the corner by the door and a stationary bike in front of the high, arched windows. "Muscle," he said, catching her looking, "keeps you going like nothing else, in my experience." He was a sinewy, shrunken, ancient man. A bottle of compressed gas and a mask sat at his elbow.

Aileen let herself be drawn to the bike, the most familiar thing in the room. It smelled of antiseptic. She didn't touch it, didn't care about the beveled console or the tablet computer mounted above the handlebars — but the view was captivating. The Fisher Building crouched above Midtown to the north, and the blue glass towers of the Renaissance Center rose head and shoulders above downtown in the same way, like two great gargoyles against the orange, citylit night, regarding each other adversarially across gentrification and passionlessly husbanded ruin. Below, even at this hour — she was trying not to look at clocks, to avoid the temptation to collapse, but it was long past midnight — automated vehicles circled in the roundabout. A digital spotlight, the source of a projected advertisement, scintillated blue and red.

"Get over it," said Beaurein, "I'm tired. I haven't got all night." He flapped a manila file folder at her until she crossed the cavernous office past the machines to his desk and took it. "You have something he wants. He's got what I want. Let's deal."

There was a chair, not a comfortable chair, but she needed it. She didn't take it. She opened the file. After adjusting to the obfuscated corporatese, she recognized it as Andrew's employee history: a bulleted list of milestones, hiring, reassignments, raises, promotions, deferments of raises and promotions. Strangely many considering the relatively short time he'd been in Detroit. It looked like a whole, life-long career, two and a half pages, printed on decadently textured paper stock of a kind she imagined was reserved for firing vice-presidents.

She sat down.

Beaurein huffed pointedly from the mask. "I took him from you, effectively. If not on purpose. I can restore him to you."

She tried to read some emotional trajectory into the pages, a process by which Andrew could have allowed this career to mean more to him than Aileen and the possibility of Christian. She'd thought of him, when she allowed herself to do so, as having been afraid of the responsibility of being a father, the loss of autonomy it entailed. The same way she'd been afraid. Was still. That he could choose this instead didn't seem real. His infectious excitement at the prospect of coming here had been short-term, short-lived — but this was ridiculous.

"You're offering to fire him? Now, after all this." She dropped the folder on the desk. "Firing him isn't going to bring him back to me."

"Not to fire him, no." Beaurein leaned back, used both his hands to lift and cross a thin leg over a thin leg. "Not sure what would happen if I did. Probably he'd disappear. No — I can make him think he wants it."

"How?"

"I've done it with the people of this city for years."

He couldn't be less than a hundred years old. When Billy Beaurein was young, some of the streets had still been paved in wood. Alcohol had been illegal. He'd lived through the Rebellion, Segregation, Jim Crow. To think of this man as a product of the same city that had produced Reg, Virgil, Gladys and Frank was like looking at the city upside down.

She wanted to snark at him, to keep up a facade of strength, for her own sake as much as Christian's. But there wasn't any strength.

Instead, Aileen watched with horror as her mind's eye presented her with the possibility. Andrew. She could have him back. A father, a partner. Resentful — secretly resentful and hating her for it. Like he had been at the end. Self-medicating to cope. A zombie, maybe. But present. Physically present, a warm body, a strength for her to lean on, to carry some of this burden she wanted and loved and needed desperately.

"I don't understand," she said.

"The hell you don't." Billy Beaurein puckered his lips. He leaned forward in his enormous synthetic leather desk chair and buzzed his secretary. "La Teesha, have Miz Dupree shown out. She's wasting my time."

It was an empty threat, he knew she knew it and didn't care, and that was terrifying enough. "I'm listening, okay? I don't know what you're talking about. What do you want from me?"

He clutched the oxygen mask to his face. "What does it look like I want?" He gestured, mask in hand, at the city beyond the windows, then at the sleek, gently glowing machines. "You know what that one is? An MRI. They got to make the goddamn thing look like a goddamn phone to justify the expense. Like I care. I go in that thing once a week to monitor the progress of my metastasis. Colon. Moving up my spine now. I want what anyone in this position wants. To go on controlling everything I can control."

"What am I supposed to —"

"What I want from you, Miz Dupree, is the Elf. The Red Elf. You know him. Don't you? You've got some in with him. More than the others. And you're new here. Vulnerable, alone. There's an angle I can work, so I'm working it. Kind of my thing. And — most important — you've got what he wants."

The Elf? She shook her head. "They don't even know I exist." She thought about that moment when she'd looked into their eyes. Had they been looking back at her or through her? "How could you possibly know what the Elf wants?"

Beaurein laughed hoarsely. "Like I said. What anyone in my position wants."

What did someone want who'd lived three hundred years to see a corporate empire and a city built and ruined and built again atop their sacred dead, who now spent their time circling and circling its streets in the middle of the night? To be left

Michael J. DeLuca

alone to mourn? A scouring of the land, and then a thousand years to pass in the blink of an eye for the forests and rivers to regrow through the concrete.

"Souls," said Billy Beaurein, like it was obvious. "That's what he wants. Unspoiled mortal souls, to join him, follow him. Like your girl. To raise in his image, then send back to destroy us."

"My ... girl?" She couldn't believe what she was hearing.

"You want to make it official? We can do that. I'm old-fashioned, I'd prefer a handshake, but I'll oblige." From a drawer he took another folder, thicker than the first. "Paperwork for a private adoption. With a fifty-thousand-dollar fee. You can have your life back, your boyfriend. You never asked for this. Who wants to be a single mother? You can go back in time. In the understanding that you'll deliver the child up to me in the person of my representative, the Red Elf, on the night of the full moon of October 31st, twenty-nine days from today. In exchange for which he, the Elf, will render unto me eternal life. It's all there, in black and white. Ironclad."

She wanted to laugh in his face, but couldn't muster the effort. She got out of there as fast as she could.

In the tropical heat outside Michigan Central Depot's colonnaded entrance, still shivering from the climate control, she mustered the resources to look up a cab company on her phone.

Grackles jabbered in the locusts as an impossibly alert Haitian opened the door of an ancient black hybrid. "Please, no air conditioning," she croaked. He laughed and opened all the windows.

When she woke, the driver was pulling the cargo bike, in pieces, from the back of the cab — front wheel, seat, chassis —

and arranging them on the curb outside Holden and Trumbull. She tipped him exorbitantly. His smile was very bright under the streetlight.

It was nearly dawn.

Inside, Omar and Morris lay spooning in her bed. Christian was in their bassinet, wide awake and so happy to see Aileen they both cried.

"That was closer than I've ever come," Morris was saying into his hands, elbows steepled on the counter above the remains of several thick slices of sourdough toast with margarine and jam. "Like I'd been climbing and climbing and then made it up onto a plateau. But it wasn't enough. I cramped, and then I was back with everybody else and you were gone."

"What did you see?" said Aileen. "Anything?"

He shook his head. "I was working so hard there wasn't a lot of room to focus, you know? But then — I came out of it completely spent, could not bear to get back on the bike. I was on Atwater, down by the river. So I went into the old hockey bar on the corner. I could barely walk that far. It was open, decently busy. There was a game on. Tom — the bartender, he's been old as long as I can remember. I swear it was him, but he was young. Younger than me. I sat there and drank two beers. I watched the people and the game and ate fries, and it felt exactly like being there with my dad when I was a kid — only *I* was my dad. It felt like a dream, but it wasn't. It was creepy. After two beers I felt totally buzzed, I was so tired. And I turned over my arm —" Morris turned over his arm, pushed up a sleeve he wasn't wearing, and touched the bare, veined muscle at the base of his elbow. "He had a tattoo. From the marines, that kind of thick ink, with the rough edges, that says somebody did it for him freehand with a hot ballpoint pen. A thunderbird drum. Like at the DIA."

"The Detroit Institute of Art," said Omar to Aileen's blank look.

Morris took a bite of toast, crunched it in his mouth, sipped the herbal tea that he and Aileen were sharing — bee balm and raspberry leaf, like breathing in a sun-scorched meadow. "Eventually I felt like I could move again, I went to pay the bill, Tom told me my money was no good. I was ready to fucking hit him. Or hug him. My dad came back to the res after war to meet his kid, heard his wife was leaving, so he pulled up roots and brought us here. Because there was work. Detroit was an industrial wasteland then, you know? Even more than it is now. Smokestacks, racism and concrete. My dad was ... an asshole. He was lost. And Tom made sure he had what he needed."

Omar looked pale, ring-eyed, sweat collecting below his mustache.

"But he wasn't real, none of it was. And I was so tired I could barely keep from falling off the stool. So I left. And then I got back on my bike and came here." Morris got up to cut himself another slice. The sound of the knife through crust was loud in the quiet, like a drunk snoring.

In their high chair slung from the counter, Christian babbled joyfully and gummed at an apple as if nothing was wrong.

"It still feels like a dream," said Aileen. All of it did, the Elf, Beaurein too. Even now, this moment, October sun angling in the windows. It was already hot again, always. "They were right in front of me," she said. "I remember their coat flapping. The city was changing around me — getting younger, older — but all from very far away. I never felt like there was any plateau, it never got easier. I don't know how I made it as far as I did." Did the Elf know she existed? Did they care? Had Virgil been there, not fighting anymore but riding easy on her beautiful brown and blue racer like he'd been born there? She couldn't remember, didn't know if it was just what she wanted to have seen.

Omar said nothing. He was by far the worst for wear for the night out of the four of them, hunched and blurry, his beard almost touching his plate. She was used to him immaculately coiffed, not a whisker out of place. She touched his shoulder. "Omar. You okay?"

"No." He shook himself, sipped at his second tiny cup of thick Moroccan coffee he'd had to go across the street to assemble. Sipped again. "I mean, Christian did great. Not exactly an angel like the way my nan talks about my niece. I think that's a front anyway. But I was pretty *fucking* scared around two when I didn't know where either of you were." She wasn't used to him swearing. "Please will you not do that again? Listen, if it's true, if Virgil's actually been with the Elf this whole time in some kind of suspended animation and not dead in a gutter somewhere, what do you think is going to happen when you catch up to them?"

"Okay," said Morris quietly. "Okay, you're right. I wasn't thinking about what it meant. I didn't know what would happen. I'm not out there trying to avenge my childhood. I was doing it because it was there, a challenge."

Aileen looked a question at him. Pleading.

He sat back. "I mean — I'm not going to stop riding. Like I said, it makes me feel connected. To the city, to this ... earth." His hand traced a circle on his arm below the elbow before he caught himself. "I just ... don't want to be my dad. Whatever that was last night, it scared me."

"Thank you," said Omar tightly.

Morris came around and hugged him. "I'm sorry," he said. After a moment Omar hugged him back, and Christian laughed, and Aileen felt relieved and happy for them, and also uncomfortably alone. She let them have their moment.

She didn't need a lover. She had friends, support, a sense of place, of belonging. She didn't want Andrew back; she wanted to have learned from having lost him, grown, gotten better. She wanted Virgil back. And she wanted to understand, if she could. If there was any kind of answer to be had about the Elf, what they meant to the city — and if Reg was right, and there was no answer but the one you made, she wanted to know that too.

"I have to try again," she said, to Christian, because they were going to be the easiest to convince, but also the most important. It was their future. "Just once more. Virgil's my friend. You guys don't know him, but he was good to us. He saved us. He was good for Noreen. I have to try to bring him back."

Then she told them about Billy Beaurein.

4

She gave herself three days to recover, time for the soreness to fade, if not completely. Time for the restlessness to return. Morris rode with her, infuriating because on his immaculately primed and tuned road bike he barely needed to pedal to keep up, scary because why, during Night Roll, had it been the other way around? She watched the sunflower gears going round on his calves. The real ones, everywhere in the gardens of the city, were drooping now, getting pecked clean by goldfinches and sparrows.

The next time it was Omar, on his utterly practical single-speed beater, because she insisted. "Are we okay?" she asked him, as soon as Morris and Christian were out of sight, Morris waving goodbye with Christian's little hand.

He kept his eyes ahead, coasting around potholes. "I'm not the one you should be asking."

"Yes, I should," she said. She felt his stiffness, she understood, but it was so exhilarating and beautiful to be moving this way again, untethered from earth, she could not so easily be made heavy. She mimicked his movements, weaving. A locust branch from a vacant lot hung low across the road, dangling leaves tinged yellow and brown from onrushing autumn and from drought. She stood on the pedals, reached for a handful that came away almost with relief. She scattered them behind her.

"I talked to Reg. She thought you knew what you're doing — but that was before. My cousin thinks you're crazy. I'm not about to ask my nan. Or my mom." A wheezing clunker rattled up behind them, filling the air with unfiltered exhaust, and Omar dropped behind her to let them pass. They waved.

He caught up easily. "I want to trust you — and I know it's not up to me anyway."

"Except it is," she said. "You want to stop me? Stop showing up to babysit."

"I'm not going to do that — I just can't understand how you could put Christian at risk."

"I won't," she said through gritted teeth and pumped until her thighs burned and her eyes blurred, trying to leave him behind.

Afterward, after she thanked Morris and Omar and got rid of them, she picked up Christian and looked into their suddenly, surprisingly attentive and intelligent blue eyes and cried and said it again. "I *won't* put you at risk. Whatever that means. I won't risk losing you. I won't risk you losing me."

She trained in the evenings, after work, before dinner, which made the rides necessarily short. Christian trained too — they had to learn not to hate the car seat or the helmet. She secured them in place and walked with them, talking about the future, about everywhere they could go when they could ride, the things they'd see. The days fell away towards Hallowe'en.

She managed the three miles, all the way back to work, to find the shop closed up for the night, Rosaria waiting outside with her own chrome and lime-green cruiser, a pair of cactus coolers, and a bag full of goodies. While Aileen caught her breath and sipped sick-sweet Mexican soda, Rosaria unzipped a tool kit and installed a battery-powered headlamp and taillight, a helmet mirror, a night-glo safety flag with the burning wheel logo in orange. Across the street, train depot traffic seemed to move in triple-time against lengthening shadows. Every time an autocar went by, gleaming mirror-windowed, Aileen's stomach clenched with dread, *knowing* it would stop, that the door would open and out would step one of Beaurein's stooges — or Billy Beaurein himself — or even Andrew. It didn't happen. Rosaria rode with her all the way back to Holden and Trumbull.

She found the Shrine of the Black Madonna on the map, and she rode there. It looked just like its picture, only in color, brown and brick and white, with newer cars going by and a sky not washed-out white but living, windswept, and roaring. It was close, so close she could have walked, and she thought of Virgil squatting alone in an abandoned house less than a mile from the church he'd gotten married in. She thought of everything she'd read about what had happened there. She remembered her dreams of churches, of double doors swinging closed when she arrived, voices echoing. The first time Virgil's shade had visited her — it felt like years ago — he'd talked about churches, all the different churches he'd ridden past, ruined and squat and ugly and vibrant and beautiful and soaring. This church had double doors like those, and she thought about going up to them, going in. But she remembered what Reg had said, and this history wasn't her own, she hadn't lived it, and its present wasn't hers either. Or else she was tired and sweaty and shy and afraid and lacked Christian's magical presence making her welcome everywhere she went. She turned her bike in the street and rode back down towards Grand.

She rode with Morris to Eastern Market, a little less than four miles, early on a Saturday when the market was just open and she could take as long as she wanted watching dew disappear from the brick with the sun, and she basked in it, this luxury that had been all she'd wanted for so long, fresh food, secured with her own money under her own power. Giddy with celebration, she overloaded the bike's cargo bed with pumpkins, apples, cider, eggplant, and squash, so much more food than she could pull on her own, but she had Morris. Together they managed, and she spent the next evenings plying Christian with little bits of pureed everything, their first real solid foods, with hilariously mixed, messy results.

She made a jack-o'-lantern. She tried to make it look like Virgil, and it just looked like a face, and she laughed, and

Christian laughed. She roasted pumpkin flesh and seeds too, and pulverized them to sprinkle over pumpkin curry, and invited Frank, Gladys, Reg and her hangers-on, Omar, his newly re-pregnant cousin and his niece, and Morris too, and they all stuffed themselves, standing or sitting at her kitchen counter, talking about babies and politics and the weather and the past and people Aileen hadn't met. It felt warm and wonderful, except that Morris kept discreetly away from Omar the whole time, she caught Omar looking at him gratefully, guiltily, and she realized they hadn't told Omar's family, and she felt bad. How could she have missed it? Yet they'd come anyway, both of them. She loved them. Conversation came around to Virgil — a trickster figure in everyone's lives, here then gone — the time he'd stolen a TV from Reg and sold it to buy her a mic — and she realized she should have invited Noreen and felt worse. She had no idea how to get in touch with him, got his number from Omar, didn't call.

The week before Hallowe'en, she rode with Morris to Belle Isle, pushing herself because it would be dark by the time she got home, and even with the headlamp and taillight and safety flag, riding at night was scary when you weren't buoyed up by music and a laughing crowd. He took her by the hockey bar where he'd spent those few hours after last Night Roll. It was busy, buzzing. The bike rack outside was full. She was struck by the sculpted, human-worn wood and brass of the door.

"Do you want to go in?" she asked when he lingered. He didn't. They just had time to coast down to the south end of the island and look at the city skyline across the water in the dusk, and then they got on their bikes again.

On the way back to Holden and Trumbull, an autocar followed them.

The night before Hallowe'en, the thunderhead to end all thunderheads rolled in and lit up the dusk like lurid casino neon for seconds at a time. Omar called and begged off dinner. "This weather — it might make people crazy. Devil's Night," he said. "It's not as much of a thing anymore, but people used to set fires in the ruins. Or anyplace they didn't like. Keeping vigil, protecting what we love, is kind of a tradition in my family." She called Morris and told him to stay home too, because she needed him not to be struck by lightning. So she spent the night before the night alone, her and Christian, sitting in the rocker watching the storm. Christian wasn't scared; they went to sleep as peacefully as if the sky wasn't being torn apart directly above their heads. Something about deep, dark sounds and the memory of the womb.

❦

In the morning, the storm had broken. In the night, the adult Christian had come to her in a dream — taller than Aileen, still blonde, sun-freckled — and told her what the world would be like. She struggled to remember, but retained only a sense of untetheredness. Doom and wild anticipation in equal measure.

When Reg and Vanessa — one of the hangers-on — arrived a little past noon, she found herself on the landing, looking up at the ladder and the trapdoor to the roof.

"Go ahead," said Vanessa, flopping down with Christian on the floor.

Of course there was a dead pot plant among the basil, mint, and tomatoes, all dead. A plastic bucket he'd been using as an ashtray, full of murk and rain. A rusted folding chair. He'd sat here, plotted abandoning her. Nothing surprising, nothing revealing. Reg had followed her up the ladder, and was salting deep breaths of rain-wet wind with puffs of weed.

The sky was ragged, full of contrasts, the kind of clouds among which any imaginable shape can be found. The rain had driven down the dust, but raised its own haze. Brick, concrete, tar, and bark glistened with rain. Puddles reflected the sky. A column of smoke rose to the southwest, and sirens blared — not an arson, Reg assured her, but a lightning strike. All the

71

leaves had been lashed from the trees. The bare branches looked hungry.

How many people out there were like Virgil? Irreverent, generous, compassionate, quixotic, poor, squatting in abandoned houses, living on takeout and bottled water, pissing down the basement stairs. How many were like Beaurein? Clutching absolutely everything within reach to their chests as they were dragged to the grave. All the displaced peoples of the world would be coming here, coming back, looking for work like Morris's dad, for room to thrive like Aileen and her fledgling, broken family, for fresh water, safety, and space to grow. They already were. Everything would change. Christian would grow weedy and tall and put down roots.

If she looked in the right direction, southwest across Holden, along the line of the rooftop, with narrowed eyes and blurred focus, Aileen could see not half-abandoned, half-vibrant city sprawl, but woods — not ancient, the furthest thing from pristine, but alive and patient. They'd weathered all. They'd resurge, like the forest of thorns that had risen from Virgil's front yard. When they did, the Elf would be waiting.

"What do I say to them?" she asked Reg.

"You mean the Elf? You can tell them to get the fuck down off that horse."

Police cars began to pass while it was still light; orange cones appeared clustered around the intersections. They were getting ready to close off the route. Marble Bar was already jumping by five, spilling out onto the sidewalk. Reg and Vanessa wished her luck, Reg hugged her, Vanessa kissed the baby, and they went across the street to sound check.

She'd forgotten the poster, the one taped to the Marble Bar's door, with a spoked moon over a stylized cityscape.

Morris and Omar had a copy when they arrived, just before dusk, dressed as a sunflower and a bee. This Night Roll wouldn't be like the others; this was the big one, when sponsorships and citywide attention made it more than a quiet gesture of community solidarity against entropy. "It'll still feel like Night Roll," said Morris. "Still weird, just bigger."

"Drunker," said Omar. "Not as kind. But I don't need to tell you to be careful."

They ate fettuccine with a walnut pesto she'd made and frozen weeks ago — a ton of it, Morris insisting she would need the carbs. Outside the triple window, long-vacant parking spaces began to fill, and costumed riders on light-festooned bikes trickled past against the normal flow. Searching for the source. Why should there be a starting point for something with no beginning or end? Somewhere, the Elf was riding towards them.

She hadn't thought about a costume. "You guys look adorable. But I'm not here to celebrate — I'm here to ride."

"Yes, you are!" said Omar, throwing up his hands. "You're celebrating six months. Christian being old enough. Having a job. Building your own cargo bike. Independence. Friends. Community. What's not to celebrate?"

She yielded, and Morris and Omar put their heads together.

Looking around at the available raw materials, which were almost entirely food, Morris suggested, "How about a harvest queen?"

She put on a cotton peasant dress, knotted at her hips to keep it away from the chain. They boiled down beet juice and chamomile greens into dye and painted her with vines and fruit running down her arms from cheeks to hands, up her ankles past her knees — a rose on Christian's cheek too, for good measure. They braided a few kale and chamomile flowers in her hair before she stopped them, laughing at her reflection in the bathroom mirror. "It's all going to come out in the wind."

She felt good, tingly, alive, seen, terrified. She shooed them out, shut the door, and counted to sixty.

Morris gathered an armload of wild red clover, chicory, and Queen Anne's lace from the vacant lots along Holden and tucked them into the car seat all around Christian. She'd practiced this with Christian for weeks, the buckles, the locking clamps, the helmet sized for a much bigger kid, thickly padded with foam to make up the difference while they grew. She spoke soothingly, explaining everything as she lifted the car seat onto the cargo bed and locked it in place.

They rode slowly up Holden towards the starting point, wherever that was. Wildflowers came loose and floated away, and Aileen watched in her rearview as Christian reached after them, tiny brows crinkling, blonde baby hair wisping in the breeze.

It was cool in the shadows, warm in the light, and the shadows got longer. The light retreated up into the trees, and then there were only shadows. Pink, green, and orange fairy lights flickered to life as riders — witches, wizards, vampires, fairies, afropunks, solarpunks — switched on their gear.

They passed a pod of night-glo Indians, and Morris got stiff.

"Nope," said Morris, to Aileen's unasked question. "We don't dress up except for powwow and the parade. And we don't dress up like *that*."

"I'm sorry," she said, looking down at the vines braiding up her arms.

Omar slowed, dropped back. Aileen watched in her mirror as he went up to them, then accelerated away, his mouth a hard line under his moustache. When he caught up, he touched Morris's shoulder.

Morris shrugged under his hand.

The flow of costumed figures on glowing bikes thickened, slowed. Streetlights came on — one or two to a block. A traffic light turned red.

Night Roll

Holden let out onto Rosa Parks and Grand in a complicated confluence of traffic islands, lanes feeding into lanes, bikes coming from three directions, cars from five. A lone cop waded into the vastness of the intersection and held up his hands, calling to mind things she'd seen in her periphery on the last moon's ride, photos she'd seen from the Rebellion, civil rights marches and before: a reporter in sneakers on a bike before a crowd, an expensive camera over his shoulder; a tank rolling down an empty street; kids playing in front of a burned-out building; boatlike Packards and Hudsons frozen in time. The cop waved bikes across from the Grand service road, and she recognized the first rider: a big, eager, older man of the spandex brewery logo school, who came often into Wheels on Fire, memorable for his size, jollity, and that he was the only member of that school she'd met who wasn't white.

He was halfway out into the intersection when an automated SUV came zipping from along Grand, accelerating not slowing, clipping his left shoulder with a mirror. He swerved and went down hard. Aileen felt as much as heard the collective gasp.

The autocar braked silently to a stop. For a moment everything was still.

Angry shouts rose from the crowd. People rushed to help the fallen rider. A naked guy in day-glo skeleton paint stepped in front of the autocar. Others joined him, surrounding the car. Among them, Aileen recognized Noreen. No costume, just Noreen.

The cop spoke into his headset.

"Oh, no," said Aileen. "Oh no." She swung her leg over and off her bike, put down the kickstand.

"What are you doing?" Omar said.

She unclipped Christian from their seat and lifted them into her arms, still in their tiny, oversized helmet, wildflowers spilling everywhere. "Come on," she said. Morris and Omar stood frozen astride their bikes. "Now!"

From opposite curbs, two other uniformed officers abandoned their stacks of orange cones and came running, drawing
weapons. The first cop drew his gun, slack-faced as if it was all
routine. Their harsh, incomprehensible commands cut
through the noise of the crowd.

Cradling Christian to her chest, Aileen jogged into the
street and stepped in front of the officers. She was shaking, her
face hot. She held Christian as far from the guns as she could,
shielding their body with hers, without taking her eyes off
those of the first officer. They were green. "Please, don't," she
told the cop in the smallest voice in the world. She was crying.
Christian was crying — screaming, terrified. "It's okay," she
told them, over and over, willing it to be true, willing herself
not to panic.

A tiny bit of tension bled out of her as she caught Morris
stepping up beside her, giant yellow paper sunflower petals
flaring ridiculously around his helmet. Omar stood further
away, a few steps past the curb, clutching the handlebars of his
beater, looking very small. Time moved slow — the opposite of
what happened with the Elf. Each individual moment was
essential, every movement and glance, and she recognized in
this stark, spotlit intensity something of Reg's interpretation of
history: how could anyone quantify this moment, whatever
came after?

After a second, Morris's fingers found hers. She squeezed
them hard.

Two people — one in a wobbly foam dinosaur suit, the
other some kind of pirate — helped the fallen rider to his feet.
A dark smear ran along the rim of his shiny white helmet.
Blood oozed from his cheek and matted his sleeve, torn open at
the shoulder. He looked dazed, head and shoulders taller than
anyone else.

Aileen felt the impulse to wave, offer to look at his bike —
she'd put so much work into it already, someone ought to at
least check the alignment — but she didn't dare move. The cop

wasn't looking at her anymore, but the eye of the gun was right there.

"I'm fine," said the injured rider thickly, looking around him at all the people who'd come to his aid. Then again, louder, "I'm fine, I'm … not pressing charges," loud enough his voice carried all the way to the pharmacy on the distant corner, to the funeral home opposite, and echoed back from the towering church ministry offices on another corner even more distant.

Christian's screams quieted at the sound, deep like thunder and also self-evidently human. Huge tears stilled on their red cheeks; their eyes were big. Their sudden calm had a palpable effect on the crowd — even on the police.

Aileen kissed their ear, just under the helmet. Everybody seemed to let out a held-in breath.

The door of the autocar opened. A man stepped out, hunched, his hands in the air. It wasn't Billy Beaurein. Some guy in shorts and expensive sunglasses. Behind him, under the dim dome light of the huge car's climate-controlled interior, sat a woman and two kids.

"Sorry," he said, speaking to the cop, not the rider. "I told the car to go. It was my mistake. I thought you were pointing at me."

Aileen did everything she could to keep still, murmuring reassurances to Christian she did not feel. She could see it all in her head going the other way, a gunshot, twenty gunshots, the blood, the crowd's reaction. It didn't.

The cop lowered his gun, holstered it. He spoke into the headset. He spoke to the driver. The driver looked at Christian, then Aileen.

The driver got back in his car. The other cops put their weapons away. One approached the injured rider, offering first aid, and was waved off. The other stood for long moments at a loss — like the rest of them — then began directing traffic.

She looked for Noreen, didn't see where he'd gone.

The river of bikes began to move. Southeast, back towards Holden and Trumbull. The tide had turned.

They found Omar pulling the last of their bikes up onto the curb, his coat-hanger-and-cellophane wings drooping. The look he gave them was brief and hollow. He spoke to the ground. "Okay," he said. "It's time. This is your chance. I'll lock my bike here and come back for it. Let me take Christian. I'll walk, meet you at home later. That way you're not putting them at risk anymore. Any more than you just did."

Christian was happy. They'd gotten one of the sunflower petals from Morris's helmet and were crinkling it and crumpling it between their fingers. Aileen was not happy, not okay. Her legs were like jelly. She sat on the curb. She couldn't take this right now. Not from Omar. It wasn't his fault.

"I don't get it," she said. "You stood up to those 'Indians.' You got right in their faces —"

"That was different. *They didn't have guns.* You could have been hurt. Christian could have been hurt."

"I had to," she said. "And I couldn't have done that without Christian. And — what would have happened if I hadn't? Nobody can know. But it would have been ... worse. And that was bad enough. Okay?"

Omar had a hand over his mouth.

Morris hugged him. "I'm ... bad at this," he said.

"Me too," said Aileen.

"I'm proud of you," said Morris into Omar's shoulder.

"Me too," said Aileen.

"I love you," said Morris.

"I love you, too," Omar said.

"You're my home, you know."

"Thank you."

And they kissed and held each other tighter, a bee and a flower, and Aileen let herself watch a second, then looked away, overflowing.

Night descended. Night Roll rolled by, still at a snail's pace, but gathering itself. Somebody had a speaker, and hip-hop boomed over the crowd, a bass line, an MC's fast, arrogant, mush-mouthed bragging about her lyrical superiority and limitless capacity for life. It was Reg.

A ragged cheer went up around them. The fallen rider was up and moving again.

"So I guess we're really doing this," Omar said with a breath.

Aileen pushed herself to her feet, found her balance. She wiped her eyes with the hem of her dress. "How am I going to find the Elf in all this?"

"He'll be at the front," said Morris. "We can get you there."

❦

They rode, single file, Morris in front ringing his bell — a single, minimalist ping, like sonar — then Aileen and Christian, then Omar bringing up the rear. The crowd let them through, gradually, in waves of laughter and conversation, song. Soon they were among people who hadn't been at Rosa Parks and Grand, hadn't seen what happened, and it could have felt like any other Night Roll. If they weren't among a thousand bikes instead of dozens.

The full moon rose in the east over the locust trees.

The wind took away Christian's sunflower petal, and they cried about it for two minutes, then got caught up in everything around them.

Passing Marble Bar, live and recorded voices of Regina the Redeemer competed. Turning onto Trumbull, there were cops again, more orange cones, and another automated car waiting, silent, blue-white headlights flaring as if with breath. The pace quickened.

It was still the finest way to see the city. Everything came together, and it all meant something more, more whole and real than anyone could take in any other way, because it came

Michael J. DeLuca

with smells, sounds, the feel of wind, with cracks, potholes and cobblestones jarring bone. Ruined churches, antique cars, gentrified boutiques, dive bars, postwar mansions, rewilded fields, renovated lofts, megachurches, artspaces, graveyards, neighborhoods bombed-out by arson or recession, "revitalized," sterilized and replaced or resurgent, still thriving. Wood smoke driven down by rain. Leaves decaying. Sulfurous vapors from deep underground. Engine fumes. Gasoline. Paint. Incense and Siberian roses. Fallen crab apples fermenting in gutters. Garbage fermenting in alleys. Dog shit. Meat slow-cooking in fat and juices. Fryer oils. Baking bread. Tortilla factories. Sweat. No wonder the Elf wanted this all the time. All of this. Aileen wanted it too.

They passed St. Anne's, walnut leaves billowing against a backdrop of brick, and burst out into the front of the pack as they turned onto Fort Street. She could see them all spread out behind her in her helmet mirror now, more coming round the corner, myriad twinkling and human, starting with Omar's worried face behind his beard. For a moment the lights of the great bridge over the river seemed an extension of the riders.

This part of Fort Street was mostly industrial, no cars in sight. Past Morris, far ahead still, she glimpsed two more riders among blank-walled warehouses, tiny against the streetlights.

She was getting tired. She'd been tired for miles, she realized. Being among the pack had made it easy not to notice.

Morris glanced at her over his shoulder. He'd lost all the petals from around his helmet. She waved. She pedaled harder. She wasn't doing this to escape from anything. She was doing this for herself, but not only for herself. She would defeat Omar's fears. She would help Virgil. She would protect Christian, she would show them something rare, and then bring them home to the real, slow, mortal world to live and thrive, to become themselves.

Ahead, the Elf's ragged coat flapped. Their long hair hung thick, threatening to tangle in the spokes. Aileen blinked, ran a hand over her eyes. Virgil was no longer struggling, relaxed in his seat, steering only with his fingertips, his knees splayed. His tracksuit looked clean. It almost glowed. He bobbed his head, as if to music. She couldn't hear. She had to get closer.

Aileen's helmet mirror was fish-eyed to give a wider view, making Christian huge in proportion to everything else. They were asleep, their head bouncing a little with the rough road. She wanted them awake. She wanted, in this moment, that look of utter faith in her. She knew there was no reaching back to touch them. Unless she stopped.

When she looked ahead again, Morris was slowing, coming level with her. He glanced over, unreadable as always, and she let herself accept that he wasn't coming with her any further. She imagined Omar riding faster to catch up, coming up on the other side, imagined how companionable and friendly that would feel, the three of them riding abreast together, even for a minute. Omar had already fallen back towards the main body of riders. Morris gave a little wave. She nodded, tears pushed from her eyes by the wind. He slowed further and was behind her. Then it was just Aileen and Christian out alone in front.

She could stop. If Christian woke and was afraid. If something went wrong.

A car idled at the stop sign on Tenth, between two blank-walled concrete warehouses. Another autocar like any of the others, not something to fear. The car pulled out between orange cones, emitting that steady, high-pitched whine meant as a warning to pedestrians. The dark shape of a cop on the corner, arms folded, looking away. Aileen pulled to the right, making way. Virgil and the Elf did no such thing, dead center in their lane. The car came uncomfortably close. She saw herself reflected in the windows as they passed under a streetlight, flowers on her cheeks, vines climbing her arms, a few leaves still caught in her hair, a spray of Queen Anne's lace from under her helmet shuddering in the wind. Mother Earth and child. She felt how fragile they both were, how exposed. The car would swerve, run them into a wall. Helmets wouldn't protect them.

A shout, and a sharp crack as something struck the tempered glass of the car's rear window. Morris had thrown something — a rock? In her mirror she saw him fishing in his pocket for another.

No light came on inside the car. No wretched, arrogant old man waved papers or pointed accusing fingers from behind glass. But she knew it was him. And simultaneously, she knew he was helpless. He wouldn't hurt her or Christian, because they were his best, terrible, stupid hope. He couldn't touch the Elf, couldn't reach them.

The autocar sped up and away down Fort Street, approaching Virgil and the Elf, then passing through them as if they were made of vapor.

"Holy shit," she heard Morris say. He put on a burst of speed and pulled closer, his front wheel aligning with her rear ones.

"It's okay," she called.

"You don't have to do this."

She shook her head. "Go with Omar," she said, panting. "He needs you."

Morris kept pace with her for a few more revolutions, then fell back.

Downtown loomed. She pulled her flask, in case this was her last chance for reprieve, and drank of the nettle tonic green and dark. She pedaled harder, muscles burning. Christian slept.

In Aileen's periphery, the warehouses began to dismantle themselves.

She blinked, and the moment her eyes were closed the world lit up like day. She could see the river, unearthly blue-white, car-sized triangles of ice jostling and cracking, a river of canines rushing south past where the international bridge once would be, then clear, white-capped, windswept, then opaque with factory farm runoff, iridescent-surfaced with petro-

82

chemical sheen. She could hear the double-stroke of her heart-beat. Fort Street rippled beneath her, spiderweb cracks spreading, healing. The street breathed, blurred with traffic, with rain. Row houses sprung out of parking lots. Outside the bus
station, a red bus with whitewalls disgorged first forty white people, then four Black people, who huddled under slanting ice waiting for their luggage until everyone else was gone. The moon sank, stars wheeled, a blanket of smoke was drawn over them and away. The Guardian Building came down brick by brick, thunderbirds and eyeless Indigenous kings receding into uncarved stone and distributing themselves to the four winds on the backs of flatbeds. Five hundred masons pulled caps low over their eyes and rode the streetcars home. The Elf didn't even roll their eyes.

She was riding with the Elf, with Virgil, riding between them, three abreast circling the Campus Martius, rolling un-hindered through cars and concrete. Pavements, monuments, and fountains shifted around them. Blood rushed in her ears.

She reached out and plucked Virgil's tracksuited sleeve. "Come back with me." Her voice as if from very far away. The fabric slipped through her fingers. She caught herself, fell back, rode harder.

A tarnished bronze general in epaulettes and cravat raised a beckoning arm before falling dead from his horse. A crowd in astonishing, roaring finery moved rhythmically outside a neon-lit theater being bulldozed in one great sweep.

"Let him go," she asked of the Elf, a different person suddenly, a woman, younger.

Entrenched Anishinaabek drove a white cavalry back across a red trickle towards a wooden fort. Old men in racist drag filed out of a club, smoking.

The bridge to Belle Isle ceased to exist as they crossed it, and they arced up and over the river's gnashing teeth and alighted among wooded marshes and spoke-wheeled cars raced by arrogant young men in goggles and scarves.

"Let all of this go," she told them, both of them, through tears, "put it down and come back to us," feeling the hollow implausibility of the request as they rounded the island's southern extremity, raising a cloud of sandhill cranes against the absent skyline, their voices a choir of door-knockers, deafening and so sudden she swerved and almost fell.

She fought to catch up.

In the moonlight, the outline of a boat, pitching in choppy surf, pulled close to the island's outer shore long enough for five hooded figures to clamber aboard through the shallows. On the wind, the scent of extinguished candles. Lights flickered on the foreign shore and were gone.

The Elf saw Aileen now, there was no mistaking it. They had changed again, a different woman, older, their eyes clear and bright. Virgil straightened, balancing no-handed now as if he'd been born to it. He craned around, nodded to Aileen, slow-smiled. Then he looked back at Christian. Their hair wisped up around the sides of their helmet. Their eyes fluttered, opened. Aileen had watched this process countless times, from sleep to waking. Virgil was missing it.

The lighthouse on the island's north point flashed through trees, answered in the lake below.

She could barely speak. "I met your son," she croaked. "Noreen. He's amazing, he plays the drums. He —" misses you, needs you. Did he? "Come back with us," she said, "come watch them grow up with me."

Her heart thudded, each breath came raw, like breathing fire. She wanted a drink, but if she reached for the flask, she would falter. The island was miles from end to end, and they'd crossed in the blink of an eye. She could keep this up a little longer. Virgil had kept it up for months. What had he seen, what had it cost him?

Stay and learn, she thought she saw him mouth.

They rounded the island and soared back across the river like birds. They rode through an old graveyard, mausolea, headstones sprouting. They rode through a cut in the path of a train; the cut undug itself with steam shovels. The Elf's face was pale under soot. They climbed up out of the earth and turned west on Canfield past a truck laden with fruit.

A house stood unchanged while trees grew from seed to tower over a cobblestone street. An elm died and fell and crushed the house next door; the other houses rotted, burned, were demolished. The yard overflowed with a forest of thorns, which was hacked away and replaced with manicured grass. A flagpole was raised on the lawn.

They pulled momentarily abreast of a bus being boarded by angry, armed men, watched an older woman help a younger woman hide on the floor at her feet, under the folds of her skirt.

Tanks rolled down Woodward.

A horse laden with beaver pelts waited, drinking from a bubbling brook. The brook turned black, paved itself over, was revealed again from beneath concrete shattered by roots, then dynamite. Sunflowers grew along its banks.

For a second, the Elf looked like Morris. They laughed at her reaction. Then, coasting beside her through time, that ancient entity sobered and became themself again, clear-eyed and worn. She would no longer be fooled by the trick that made their lined face seem a mask. They were too alive. They nodded to her — no, towards Christian — a jerk of the head, a conspiratorial quirk of brow. Panting, heart in throat, the veg- etable dyes on her skin running with perspiration, not knowing how she was able to keep this pace — yet keeping it — Aileen was so astonished at this acknowledgment of her presence that she almost missed the substance of it. The Elf, who for all Reg's efforts to undermine her own story couldn't be less than four hundred years old, who was uncontestably far, far older — thousands on thousands — who had witnessed the glaciers, the entire transformation of this place *and consented to share it,* was playing with her, joking. All the hallucinations and insomnia, the grief and loneliness rational and irrational, hadn't meant nothing. She was more than a mother, a cast-aside lover — more than herself? She'd already been changed by what she'd seen. That process wasn't finished. Everything Virgil had done in secret to achieve this, to reach this place — he was a little like the Elf already. She, an outsider, gentrifier, had been offered the same chance.

Souls: that was what Billy Beaurein thought the Elf was seeking in circling the city like this, drawing a caravan of fairy-touched mortals behind them over miles, through months and years. Was he wrong? Did it matter?

Aileen followed the Elf's gaze, looking behind her into the fish-eye helmet mirror that had been a gift from Rosaria, and with horror, realized she didn't recognize her own baby.

Against the backdrop of a storm-lit, ancient, future city, there was someone in the car seat, wide-eyed and calm — but not someone she knew. It *was* Christian. But they were changing, growing older even as she watched, their hair thickening, darkening, their face changing, becoming less a baby's, more a child's.

"No," she said, gasping. "Wait, don't —"

The rush of time, this torrent of experience — it was wonderful, *being* the city, she wanted more. Virgil was right, he had been right to fight his way here, to quest for this, and she couldn't be the one to take it from him. But for Christian, who'd had only six months in which to learn the shapes of so few faces, who couldn't read the books she and Virgil had read, who hadn't been hurt the ways Aileen, and Virgil too, had been hurt? She couldn't ask this of her child. She didn't want them to grow up this way, in this rushing limbo of pain, of constant change. There had been times — lots of times, feeding in the middle of the night, dead exhausted in the blinding afternoon, when she'd wished she could fast-forward, fall asleep and wake and be past it. Now that she'd survived it, she didn't want that anymore. She couldn't even want it taken away now that she'd lived it. She didn't want to miss anything. She wanted every laugh, every fall, every cry. Even maybe one in three squirming impossible diaper changes. She couldn't let it slip past.

All she had to do was stop pedaling. She barely even had to do that.

"I can't," she told them both. "I'm sorry."

A casino loomed bloody pink against the sky and was obscured by a chorus of smokestacks. The Elf's face was a mask. Virgil reached for her hand. She reached for his, but the space between their outstretched fingers did not close, it widened.

❦

Aileen fell from the Elf's wake. She coasted beneath a ragged gray sky, past clapboard Victorians that disintegrated and re-solved into high-fenced brick projects, then had to slam on the brakes as Calumet ended abruptly at the freeway guardrail. Virgil and the Elf sailed on away from her, over the freeway, through empty air, and into trees on the other side. It started to rain. Her chest heaved. She dismounted and pulled Christian out of the car seat restraints. They were no heavier than she remembered, no bigger. But something had changed about their face, sallow in half-light, a mask of fear. Holding them, she sank onto the broken curb, sobbing to breathe. Her pulse roared. Cars whooshed past on the M-10 below, washing both of them in windborne grit.

Her stomach growled and snapped.

Aileen didn't know if it was dusk or dawn.

She leaned her head against the guardrail and felt, if not for Christian, she would melt and be subsumed into the pavement like all those abandoned bikes everywhere across the city.

It started to rain.

An autocar pulled to a faintly whining stop in front of her and hulked there, unmoving, for a span of immeasurable time, rain plinking and beading on the windows, while Aileen couldn't even distantly convene the energy to react. A rear door opened; someone in a suit, not Andrew, got out with a phone to their ear. Aileen compelled her clay muscles to pull her to her feet. She planted the strange Christian back in their seat, fitted the restraints over their now-rigid limbs as they began silently to scream. With searing pain, she managed to swing her leg over the seat. She stood on the pedals and got the bike rolling away. The car pursued her at a crawl, but she was too devastated, too spent and hungry to care or even notice when it gave up the chase and disappeared. Billy Beaurein would die withered and bitter. The parts of the city and the people he'd poisoned would go on, self-perpetuating, until there was nothing left. Until then, life would go on too.

There were no lights on in any of the buildings, no shops or restaurants. This part of the city, like her own, was a desert, built for cars not people.

The casino sent up a dull beacon. Always open. She pedaled two miles before she reached it. It was all she could do not to fall from the saddle.

She went in past the soaring 3D-printed plastic copy of the Spirit of Innovation, past the poker tables, into an impossibly gleaming-new chrome diner. She ordered grits, rye toast and a banana smoothie, then fries and french onion soup, then chamomile tea with pesticide corn syrup "honey." She devoured everything, with Christian looking on from a high chair in a daze.

They would never be the same. Which future Christian from her dreams and visions would they become? Not any. They'd grow up different, far-eyed and quiet, but surrounded by the love of friends and strangers. Like Noreen?

Her phone had no charge. She plugged it in, waited 'til it came alive. Three days had passed. Three days. Only three. It was dawn, not dusk. Outside it would be getting lighter, though there were no windows, just paintings of windows with the city in them. Eventually, she'd call Noreen and tell him the whole story. Tell him she was sorry.

She called Omar.

"You were right," she told him.

"Stay there," he said, "we're coming." She imagined them untangling themselves from her bed.

She caught her reflection in chrome: her hair wild with exhaust, seeds, smoke, and sweat, damp with rain, her skin smeared with vegetable dyes. Mother Nature.

TVs flickered silently overhead; the radio played Motown, Martha and the Vandellas' "Nowhere to Run." Aileen held Christian's tiny hand in hers and fed them spoonfuls of banana smoothie, singing along with every word, until finally they smiled.

Acknowledgments

Thank you, Selena Middleton, for taking such care of this book and making it better. Thanks to Marissa Lingen and Desirina Boskovich for their enthusiasm and support. Thanks to Gavin Grant and Scott Andrews for their example and counsel. Thank you to the staff and contributors of *Reckoning* for giving me a context and community from which to build these ideas. And to the new parents of Detroit, and everywhere, thank you for wanting to do the work of raising new lives into this future.

About the Author

Michael J. DeLuca lives in the rapidly suburbifying post-industrial woodlands north of Detroit with partner, kid, cats and microbes. He is the publisher of *Reckoning*, a journal of creative writing on environmental justice. His short fiction has appeared in *Beneath Ceaseless Skies, Apex, Mythic Delirium*, and lots of other places.

STELLIFORM PRESS

Earth-focused fiction. Stellar stories.
Stelliform.press.

Stelliform Press is shaping conversations about
nature and our place within it. Check out our
upcoming titles and articles and leave a comment or
review on your favorite social media platform.

Lightning Source UK Ltd.
Milton Keynes UK
UKHW011841101020
371362UK00001B/157